THE DARK SIDE OF THE HEART

Following the death of her parents in an accident, Jean Sinclair travels from the US to Scotland to trace her family roots, despite disapproval from her fiancé, Don. There, she meets Adam Crawford, a handsome but arrogant landowner. Despite herself, Jean falls for Adam — only to be cruelly rejected. Broken-hearted, she flies back to Texas, only for Don to treat her with sudden and terrifying harshness. Adam follows her to America, where the two men confront each other violently, and Jean has to face the possibility that her parents' deaths may not have been accidental after all . . .

Books by David Wiltshire
Published by The House of Ulverscroft:

THE TEARS OF AUTUMN
THE WOUNDED HEART
SCENT OF MADNESS

DAVID WILTSHIRE

THE DARK SIDE
OF THE HEART

Complete and Unabridged

ULVERSCROFT
Leicester

First published in Great Britain in 2012 by
Robert Hale Limited
London

First Large Print Edition
published 2014
by arrangement with
Robert Hale Limited
London

The moral right of the author has been asserted

A catalogue record for this book is available
from the British Library.

ISBN 978–1–4448–1825–3

Published by
F. A. Thorpe (Publishing)
Anstey, Leicestershire

Set by Words & Graphics Ltd.
Anstey, Leicestershire
Printed and bound in Great Britain by
T. J. International Ltd., Padstow, Cornwall

This book is printed on acid-free paper

For Eileen Pickering
Thanks for the encouragement

1

The entrance to the loch was a strip of wild water. Far out to sea the huge Atlantic rollers began to break at their tops as they bore in towards the great headland, where the sheer cliff dropped over a hundred feet into the white, boiling foam. When each surging wall of green water struck the rocks, the earth vibrated and great lumps like candyfloss detached from the foam and flew up the cliff face and out across the dead brown heather. Miles inland, in the shelter of the mountains, the fury was gone, the water of the loch calm, tranquil, giving no hint of the wild beauty and raw strength of nature so close at hand.

Had she been able to look into the future the young woman at the window of a turreted castle might have recognized the similarity between herself as she then was, with the silent, tranquil loch she was gazing down upon, contrasting with the woman she would become, the woman of the plunging sea beyond her vision.

It was the first day of Jean Sinclair's holiday; the first day in fact, that she had really set eyes on Scotland. Last night when she had arrived by coach from the airport, where she had flown in from America, it had been pitch black. She had heard so much about it from her mother back home in Wichita Falls, Texas, about how green it was, and how friendly the people were, that she could hardly believe she was really here, standing in a room of a converted castle that was older than any building in the town she had been raised in, indeed in the entire United States.

Inverdee Hotel was set in acres of woods and moorlands that swept down to the water's edge. A wooden pier pointed like a finger across the loch to the village of Inverdee itself, the place where her mother had been born and raised and had only left when she had married her 'Yank'. Pop had been in the American Airforce stationed in England, up on a fishing trip when they had met and fallen in love, a real whirlwind romance. Jean had been born ten months later in Germany, her father's next posting. Three years on, the family had moved back Stateside, to Sheppard AFB at Wichita Falls. It had become their permanent home on his retirement from the service. And now, unbelievably, they were dead, killed in an automobile wreck on the Interstate Highway. Even now, months later, Jean felt the lump come instantly into her throat, and her eyes filled with tears.

It had happened last Fall, and it was while she was going through her mother's things, seeing again old photographs of the beautiful young woman she had been, that she had conceived the sudden urge to see her mother's birthplace. Don, her fiancé had been, to say the least, unhelpful, in fact downright difficult. All right, so it was only two months to their wedding day and there were a lot of things still to do, but she had been, was still, very upset by his lack of sensitivity under the circumstances. He couldn't see how important it had suddenly become to her to find her roots at this very tragic, emotional time in her life.

But that was the norm for men, so her far more experienced friends had told her. The truth was, Jean had led a somewhat sheltered life, and in matters concerning the opposite sex was positively naive. But she had no real regrets about that, and having trained as a nurse and seen the sometimes terrible consequences of casual sex, she was glad she was still a virgin at her age. To be fair to Don, if she had given in to his demands, and slept with him because, as he put it, they were 'almost there now', he might have been more reasonable about her coming away for a month. Or would he?

She thought again of Don. He was handsome, the proverbial tall, dark and handsome, or rather, in his case, tall, blond and handsome, with ice-blue eyes.

They had met at college, where he played for the football team. She had not made it to the cheerleaders' squad — she was too quiet and retiring for that — but all the same he had asked her out on a date, much to the amazement of all the other girls, and herself. She had never swooned at his feet like some of them, and she had no idea how attractive she was to men.

They had dated on and off until the end of the term, then he had gone off to Dallas to study accountancy and Jean had started her nursing training.

So it was a shock when he had looked her out on his return. He had courted her slowly, with old-world charm and southern courtesy, bringing her flowers, and gifts for her parents, and at the beginning never putting her under pressure to 'go all the way'. He could be real fun, and generous, but at other times, as the months had passed, harsh and rather rough with her. He was a big man, and didn't know his own strength.

Once, when they'd started to have a row, he'd grabbed her upper arm and forcibly marched her from the restaurant where they'd been having a meal with friends — or at least his friends.

She'd been laughing with a guy called Al, and Don had got jealous. He was prone to that, especially when he had been drinking.

She'd talked a lot to Al because she didn't have much in common with the girls in the party, and in fact she had formed the opinion that they thought of her as a stuck-up bitch, not into excessive drinking — she'd seen the results of it in her hospital work — or doing a lot of the things they liked doing, such as excessive shopping. That was because she didn't have a lot of surplus cash after she'd helped out her parents; after all, they'd kept her through her training. Sometimes she wondered what Don saw in her; they shared so few interests.

Her parents hadn't liked Don, and she knew that, even before her mother had seen the bruises on her arm where he had held her so tightly.

She knew that they thought she could have done better for herself — a doctor, perhaps.

The bruising had caused a blazing row, and although things had quietened down after he had apologized to her and said it would never happen again, and was always on his best behaviour in front of her parents, she knew they had never really liked him.

But when they had died Don had been marvellous; if only they could have seen how comforting and affectionate he'd been.

Jean swallowed. How hard life could be. They'd never seen the gentle, good side of him.

Now Don was all she had — that and the photographs she'd been going through in her mother's things.

That was why she was here — to see where her mother had come from — her *roots*.

She reckoned most of Don's problems were her fault, because she continued to insist that they wait until they were married before she gave herself fully to him.

Of course, there had been moments, as she was sure every woman had experienced at some time in their life, when she felt the frisson of danger of the unknown, and the excitement that came with stepping outside their safety zone.

It had happened several times just before her parents had died, when he had come on strong, but always she stiffened, stopped him, and clearly he was feeling more and more frustrated.

For that she felt a terrible guilt.

But for her, it was a matter of principle.

And since the loss of her parents, now,

more than ever, she wanted to be like her mother on *her* wedding day.

A virgin.

Lately, he'd only ever taken her out when there was a gang of them, never on their own. She couldn't remember the last time that had happened.

It was flattering that he liked to show her off, but just the once would have been nice. Sometimes they had started that way, but inevitably they always seemed to bump 'accidentally' into a couple of friends whom he insisted on buying a drink, and she was left on the sideline, wearily waiting for the time to go home. Men were selfish by nature, she had noted. They did what they liked, when they liked; fished, went to football matches and drank with their buddies as and when it pleased them. Don was no different from the rest of them in that regard.

Selfishness and not paying her attention was one thing, but when she had announced her intention of taking this trip, he had become very difficult, even aggressive.

He'd really tried hard to stop her, and when that had failed, he'd thrown a huge sulk as she continued to stick to her guns.

And it seemed so awful because you'd have thought he'd have been more attentive and

7

considerate now that she was alone in the world.

Certainly, her parents would have been horrified at the way he'd tried to bully her out of coming.

It was as if he was bordering on paranoid possessiveness.

But the more he'd put the pressure on, the more determined she had become, even amazing herself.

Just a couple of days before she was due to depart he'd disappeared completely, without telling her he was making one of his frequent business trips. When he'd finally reappeared it seemed as though he was reconciled to her going, though was still by no means happy about it.

And instead of taking her to the airport he'd arranged a taxicab.

Jean had been left feeling very upset, had thought long and hard about their relationship, but had come to the conclusion that all it showed was that Don loved her very much; it was just because he couldn't bear to think of her being away. Well, no doubt all that would pass when they were married.

Guilt got her again. It was all her fault, really. At the bottom of it was, no doubt, the fact that she was denying him what all his buddies were undoubtedly getting regularly.

It was then a thought struck her. She couldn't believe her naivety.

Maybe he was seeing somebody when he was on his business trips — that's why he had put up with her until now. He was so handsome, so popular that he could easily fix himself up with one-night stands.

Jean frowned. Was that supposed to make her feel better? Did his buddies know? Did their *girlfriends* know? She must be a laughing stock.

Jean felt her cheeks burning. When she got back home she would have to challenge him, it would be unbearable not to know the truth.

But it was still her responsibility for being so old fashioned and unfair to him.

Well, he wouldn't have to wait long now. She consoled herself that once they were married, things would be different — he would be different.

Don would go back to being that uncomplicated guy she had first met.

But she still worried about the future. When he was middle-aged, beset with life's difficulties, would he go the same way as his miserable, overbearing father?

She turned away from the window, conscious that she was avoiding the issue, and began showering then climbed into jeans topped off with a lime-green cashmere sweater. She knew it complimented her eyes and went well with her auburn hair, which fell in a wild tangled mass to her shoulders. Jean began to attack it with even more than her customary vigour, excited and anxious to get down to breakfast, but it stubbornly refused to come to order. In exasperation she tied it back and then proceeded to apply the minimum of lipstick and eyeliner. With her feet pushed into comfortable loafers, Jean grabbed her shoulder purse, remembering they called it a handbag over here, and made her way down the fine big staircase.

The dining room was huge with three double French doors leading out onto the terrace with its statues and flower tubs reminiscent of Italy, especially with the view of the distant mountains.

'Good morning, madam.' Jean winced at the formality, but revelled in the lovely Scots accent of the smiling fresh-faced girl of her own age.

'Hi, please call me Jean.'

The girl looked taken aback and shot a quick glance in the direction of an older woman who was obviously in charge of the restaurant. 'How many is it for — ' she hesitated for a fraction before adding with a shy smile — 'Jean?'

10

'Just me. Have you got a table near a window?'

The girl picked up a menu from the reservation desk and led the way.

'There you are.' She pulled aside a chair and Jean slipped into it.

'Tea or coffee?'

Jean chuckled. 'I've heard about the coffee over here, perhaps I should go for the tea?' The girl jotted it down on her notepad.

'And will you require porridge first?'

'Good heavens!' Jean's hand went to her stomach, 'What are you trying to do to me?'

The girl looked down at the friendly American and pulled a face. 'I don't think you've got anything to worry about.'

Jean snorted. 'Don't you believe it.' She glanced at the menu and then snapped it shut. 'But I can't resist the scrambled eggs and bacon, especially if somebody else is cooking them.'

'Very well.' The girl turned to go, but Jean said, 'And what's your name?'

The shy smile flittered across her face again. 'It's Kath.'

'Do you come from around here, Kath?'

'Yes, I'm from a little village down the road.'

Delighted, Jean couldn't help but say, 'My mother came from here, married my father and went to live in the States. We never visited; this is my first time over here.'

Kath put her head on one side, and said in her cute Scots accent, 'What was your mother's maiden name then, Jean?'

'Anderson, but my grandparents died some time ago and I don't think there is anybody left around here, Grandfather came up from Glasgow during World War Two.'

'Was your grandmother a local girl?'

The question took Jean by surprise.

'Yes — yes she was.' She frowned. 'Let's see, her name was . . . Johnson. That's right, Fiona Johnson. Do you know anyone with that surname?'

The girl's hair swished around her shoulders as she shook it.

'Sorry — I can't help you there.'

When Kath had bustled away with the order, Jean sat looking out of the open French doors, past the stone balustrade to the rooftops of Inverdee, just visible at this lower level above the trees beyond.

It was true her mother had never spoken much about her family's past, always life in the village in terms of her mum and dad and the fun they had. Up to now Jean had never thought about it, and even with her recent urge to come back she hadn't given any great thought about the family tree. Roots to her had simply meant a sentimental journey into her immediate past, that which she had heard about from her mother. Yet a chance remark by Kath, Jean realized, had put a wholly different complexion on her visit.

With sudden insight Jean knew that there was a mystery. Never, she now realized, had there been any talk of her great grandparents on the distaff side, only about her grandfather's folk on Clydebank. Why in all those years had her mother never said anything about her family history — after all this was a very romantic part of the world what with the clans and the mountains.

Kath came back with her tea and some toast. 'There you go.' She made to turn but Jean said quickly, 'Pardon me, but where would I go to find out about my grandmother's folks?'

'Ooh,' Kath's face screwed up in thought. 'I'm not very good at things like that, but I could ask Mrs McPhearson.' She glanced in the direction of the woman in charge. Jean got the impression that Kath wasn't overly keen to do so, and the room was beginning to fill with people, so she said quickly, 'No, don't worry, I'll check it out with reception.'

While she sipped her tea and buttered her toast Jean observed her fellow guests, nodding to the occasional person she

13

recognized from the airline and bus of the previous day. They were mostly Americans on a package vacation as was she, except she had purchased an extra week. Money, as always, was tight and with the wedding and everything it increased her feelings of guilt. Poor Don was probably even now working away in one of his father's stores. She allowed herself a chuckle; if you could call it work. Don had pretty liberal hours, especially compared to the shifts she had to work.

While she waited she looked around the fine big room, smiling at several elderly couples she had met on the journey over.

There was also a couple of younger guys — in their mid-forties — who had been on the flight but who were not part of the tour party.

They'd started to talk to her the moment she had found her seat when they were boarding, one helping to lift her luggage into the overhead locker, before sitting across the aisle from her; the other holding out his hand.

'Hi there, I'm Chris, and this ugly fellah is Steve.'

She took it, noticing its hardness as she smiled and said, 'Jean.'

They were big, well-built men, and told her they were from Dallas.

They'd decided to take a break — lucky to get their seats at the last moment.

Jean had chatted enthusiastically to begin with, thrilled with the prospect of her trip, talking about the places she was going to see.

It turned out that they were going to Scotland for the fishing, after salmon in the Highland rivers, and were not part of the holiday group. They'd just joined for the flight and accommodation because it was a good deal.

She was disappointed at first, since they certainly would have entertained the tours and visits, but as the hours passed she had, vaguely at first, then with increasing certainty, realized that they were hitting on her.

After that she tried reading, or pretending to be asleep, but she was still aware that they were continually looking in her direction.

When the final meal was served, she had to talk again.

They helped her with her luggage, getting a trolley and lifting her cases from the carousel, but on boarding the bus she sat next to a widowed lady from Houston, the two opposite seats already occupied. They had to walk past, further towards the back.

They were decent enough guys, friendly and helpful, but she had no interest in a holiday 'romance' as they were euphemistically called.

That had been another occasion she had wondered about her sexuality. Girls were so liberated these days, could control their own fertility and not depend on a man. That they enjoyed this freedom like they never had in any generation before, right back to Eve, made her wonder why she was so old-fashioned.

Was it the way she had been raised by loving, conservative parents?

It was not uncommon for many girls in the Bible belt to be virgins at their marriages, but she had no deep religious feelings to fall back on — no excuse, if you wanted to call it that.

So, was it something else? Was she just naturally . . . cold?

Poor Don, perhaps things would never be right for them.

Suddenly, snapping back to the present, she realized Chris had got up and was coming over to her table.

'Hi there Jean — sleep well?'

His dark eyes roamed over her, full of amused suggestiveness, but not in the least bit threatening. Given half a chance, though, she guessed he would take it.

'Yes thank you Chris, and you?'

He leaned over her, fists on her table.

'With this glorious fresh air — you betcha. Looking forward to a day's fishing. We're going to meet our gillie this morning, get the lowdown from him.'

Jean frowned.

'What's a gillie?'

He told her of the traditional help on the Scottish Estates, the nurturing and expertise these men had. Made all the difference to your vacation, apparently.

Jean thought to herself that there was so much to learn about her mother's country.

They were joined by Steve, whom she'd seen out of the corner of her eye, standing up and finishing his coffee before coming over to them.

'Morning, Jean.'

She smiled up into his face with its slightly pockmarked cheeks. It gave him a tough, very masculine look that sent a shiver down her back, but when he smiled his face crinkled up in a most attractive way.

'Hi there, Steve, you had a good night too?'

He nodded, and then gestured in Chris's direction.

'I could hear him snoring through the wall.'

The latter frowned and straightened up, shot his friend a mock withering look.

'Oh yeah, what about your annoying habit

of singing in the bathtub — drives me crackers.'

He looked back down at her.

'You got anything on today, Jean? If not, would you like to come with us? We'll show you how to fly-fish.'

Jean smiled, shook her head.

'That's kind of you, but I'm going on an overnight trip — it's part of our package.'

Jean was thankful she had a ready-made excuse; the last thing she wanted to do was stand in some icy godforsaken stream with two very masculine men in their prime of life.

The first, escorted, outing was an all-day tour of the West Coast, with an overnight stay at a hotel in Oban, so that they could take a steamer to Fingal's Cave and the holy isle of Iona.

It was going to be a marvellous trip, and Jean was very excited by the prospect, but she couldn't deny the frustration that she had to wait a little longer to see the place where her mother had grown up and where her parents had met and married — tantalizingly close as it was.

She had thought of ducking the various trips included in the price, especially one to Glasgow with a performance of the opera *Tosca* in the evening. She had no idea why that was on the itinerary but presumed it was to showcase Scottish Opera and Orchestra, and the arts in general, since it included a visit to a gallery.

But she had dismissed the idea because, frankly, there would be plenty of free days towards the end of the week, and the extra time she had paid for.

Besides, it would be nice to set her family's story into the whole of the Scottish Experience.

'Oh well, perhaps another time.'

They grinned in unison.

'See you later then,' said Chris.

Jean smiled.

'Not until tomorrow evening — at dinner. Have a nice day now.'

She looked at their retreating backs, wondered if they were married or not. She hadn't noticed any wedding rings, but then not all men wore them.

Further thoughts were interrupted by the arrival of her eggs and bacon.

'Mm, these smell real good.'

Kath gave her a sly smile. 'There's fried bread as well.'

It was a substantial plateful and Jean's face must have shown her concern because Kath added quickly, 'You'll need it for energy for the dancing.'

'Dancing?'

'Yes, traditional country dancing — it's in your brochure for Saturday night.' She chuckled, 'They call it a Highland Ball.'

Jean had been so full of excitement about her mother's past that she only vaguely remembered the booklet with its colourful picture of men in kilts and dark evening-style jackets, the women in long dresses with tartan sashes. 'Good heavens! I can't do that.'

Kath shook her head dismissively. 'Of course you can, everybody joins in. The staff come in especially for the occasion to help out, and the Highland people from Inverdee always send a team to demonstrate. They show you what to do — it's very popular.'

Jean thought about it and became quite taken with the idea. It would be enormous fun, and with the locals present a great opportunity to talk about her family's past. Then a frown crossed her face. 'But hang on, I haven't got anything to wear remotely like the dresses in the picture.'

Triumphantly Kath said, 'You really didn't read your brochure very thoroughly, did you? The hotel has a large collection of full-length evening-wear they loan free of charge for the night, like they do for the medieval party.'

'Well in that case I can hardly say no, can I?'

Jean picked up her knife and fork and cut some of the bacon. 'You will be there as well, won't you, Kath?'

The girl looked around guiltily; she had stayed talking longer than she should have. 'I was supposed to be going with my boyfriend to a football match he's in, but if you'd like me to come I'd rather be here.'

Delighted, Jean put her knife down and gave Kath's hand a quick squeeze. 'That's great, we'll have us some fun.'

She forked in a mouthful of the bacon as, grinning, Kath gave an exaggerated appraisal of Jean's seated form. 'As soon as I've finished here I'll go to the housekeeper and sort out a couple of dresses for you and leave them in your room — they go so quickly later. Don't worry if you don't like them. I won't be offended if you're wearing something different on the night, but at least you'll have a chance at something decent.'

'Bless you, Kath, I don't know how I'd have managed without you.'

Mrs McPhearson's rock-like face suddenly heaved into view. 'Is anything the matter, Miss Kirk?'

Quickly Kath moved away saying, 'Not at all, Mrs McPhearson, I was just giving the lady some directions.'

Jean gave the woman a curt, dismissive nod

and picked up her knife again, fearful that Kath might get a ticking off for being slow or something. She was really pleased and excited at the way they had hit it off together so quickly.

Jean finished her meal and ran back up to her room, hurriedly brushed her teeth, packed her toilet bag into her overnight case, together with spare underwear and a top, and was downstairs again and outside breathing in the soft, moist, *clean* air that was so very different from what she was used to, all inside five minutes. As she passed the French windows, feet crunching on the gravel, she saw Kath inside clearing a table. Jean gave a cautious, secretive little wave and got one in reply, conscious that they were acting rather like schoolgirls dodging teacher — the formidable Mrs McPhearson. Somehow that made their new-found bond even closer.

The bus was parked outside the main entrance. A little group of her fellow travellers were milling about the guide, and the driver was already waiting patiently in his seat, the diesel engine ticking over.

Jean gave her name, and was ticked off the guide's checklist.

'Here, let me help you with that.'

She turned to find Chris reaching out his hand and picking up her small case she'd set down on the gravel.

'Oh, that's kind of you — but it's not heavy.'

He placed it into the open side of the bus's luggage area.

Chris shook his head of dark curly hair. 'No problem. I'll see you tomorrow then.'

He crunched away on the gravel to a rental 4×4 that Steve was loading with rods and tackle. He waved to her. She waved back and called out, 'Hope you catch a lot,' then boarded the bus.

From her high-up seat in the coach she waved again as they backed up, then drove away, Steve's elbow showing out of the driver's window.

The bus finally got underway, lumbering out of the entrance gates and down the narrow lane. She had a clear view of the hotel's green lawns sweeping down to the loch-side landing stage.

The boat that plied across the water to Inverdee wasn't there. Later, between the passing trees, she had fleeting glimpses of the far side of the loch, and the rooftops of the little place that meant so much to her.

On impulse, she almost got out of her seat to approach the guide sitting beside the driver, to ask her to stop the bus and let her out, but even as she put her hand out to the back of the seat in front to hoist herself up, the bus reached a larger road, turned left away from the direction of Inverdee and picked up speed.

Resignedly, she sagged back into her seat and winced at her reflection in the window.

It was too late now so she might just as well get on with it and enjoy the next couple of days.

Which she did.

When the bus finally reached their overnight stop, it was to find the small, bustling town of Oban had a fine wide harbour full of ships of all shapes and sizes.

She slept well that night, and arose ahead of the main party. After breakfast she went out, crossed the road and stared out over the anchorage.

It was a brilliant morning with only a slight breeze gently fluttering the flags outside the hotel. Seagulls screeched and fought for the scraps near the stern of several ships.

Around about were the low hills and beyond, the mountains of this beautiful coast. It was so, so, different from Texas.

She wondered which boat they would be taking.

In the event, it turned out to be a brightly painted, old-fashioned-looking steamer, with a dark blue hull, white upperworks and a dark funnel with the air above it shimmering with the heat from the engine.

Soon they were churning the water, leaving a white wake as they headed out down a long sea loch.

The highlight for her was when they clambered down an outside set of ladders into a small outboard craft that took them into Fingal's Cave on Staffa, with its staggering, cathedral-like vault formed by the soaring pillars of rock.

They then went to the holy island of Iona and its abbey, where Jean really began to sense, for the first time, the ancient civilization that had lived for centuries on this rugged, magnificent land.

They finally arrived back at Oban, and boarded their waiting bus. It was four o'clock before they got underway, climbing out of the town, the labouring engine vibrating the bus. She looked back, out of the window, knowing that somehow, a part of her belonged here, had always been here.

It was a strange feeling, almost as if . . . as if . . . She shook her head, puzzled. Almost — almost, as if she was another woman.

Jean closed her eyes, suddenly exhausted, and went almost immediately to sleep.

They finally arrived back at the hotel as the sun was setting, a fiery red ball slipping down behind the dark mass of the mountains, only the flash of tumbling streams showing their steep, precipitous sides.

As she stepped down onto the gravel and walked towards the hotel entrance, with its inviting warm lights and sparkling chandeliers she passed Chris and Steve's mud-spattered 4×4.

Clearly they had been down by a river, all right. She wondered how they had got on.

There was just time for a quick shower before she changed into a skirt and blouse, and with a cardigan over her shoulders, tripped down the stairs, hungry for supper.

As she passed the crowded bar a voice called out, 'Jean — over here.'

They were perched on bar stools, glasses of beer and scotch before them.

She hesitated, but Chris, dark eyes beaming, slid off his stool and waved for her to come over.

'Join us for a drink.'

Reluctantly, she made her way towards them. The 'boys' were nice enough, in fact good fun, but she really didn't want to get involved with them, or anybody else for that matter, but she didn't want to be rude, either.

'What'll it be?'

She looked at their glasses on the bar. Jean wasn't much of a drinker, really, but she did have the occasional glass of wine with a meal.

'Oh, a white wine — thank you.'

Chris turned to catch the barman's eye as Steve said, 'How did your trip go?'

'It was wonderful.'

They hardly got a word in edgeways as she prattled on about what she had seen, and then suddenly realized what she was doing.

She stopped, took a sip of the cold wine she had been given and said, 'Sorry, I must be boring you both stupid.'

Chris chuckled. 'No, no, it sounds terrific.'

There was, unusually, a pause, which she suddenly filled with, 'Oh, and how did you guys get on?'

They looked at each other with exaggerated dismay, then Chris groaned.

'Didn't catch a thing. I'm not sure there's even any fish in these rivers.'

Steve's pockmarked cheeks caught the reflected light of his cut-glass tumbler as he tossed back his whisky, took a pull of beer, then ran the back of his hand across his mouth before saying, 'I reckon it's a local con trick. These Highland laddies know what they're doing — better than any Maddison Avenue Advertising Agency.'

Jean winced, not wishing to believe anything bad about her new-found love of all things Scottish.

'Oh, surely not?'

Steve pressed his lips together into a tight line and shook his head slowly.

'Costs a bomb, too. I reckon we'd have done better in Canada.'

Chris snorted. 'Talking of bombs, perhaps we should try dynamite tomorrow.'

'Good idea.'

Horrified, Jean was about to protest when she suddenly saw the twinkle in their eyes.

'Oh you guys, You're putting me on.'

They broke into hoots of laughter.

'Don't worry, Jean, we just love it here.'

With that, Chris waved to get the barman over again, pointed at the empty whisky glasses, then turned to her.

'Join us for dinner.'

They were handsome, rugged, good fun, exuding a worldly-wise charm, but Jean really wanted to be on her own.

And besides, she didn't want them to think she was leading them on.

She lied. 'That's good of you, but I rather promised a lady on the bus we'd dine together tonight. She's a little lonely.'

Steve scratched his dimpled chin.

'Aw, that's a shame. Another night, perhaps?'

'Yes — that would be great.'

She wondered how long she could keep up the excuses. Tomorrow would be okay as the group she was with were off to Glasgow, evening meal included, and would be back late. They took their replenished glasses, held them up in a toast to her, clinked them all together, before downing theirs in one go, followed by more beer.

Jean's face must have looked concerned because Chris winced, and said apologetically, 'It's the job. When we're off duty we play hard — it helps.'

Intrigued, she asked, 'Job? Is it that stressful?'

They looked at each other, and then Chris put on a stern face and mimed a tough movie voice.

'We're cops — Dallas, and what's a good looking broad like you doing in a dive like this?'

Steve joined in.

'Book her, Dano,' then he hummed the *Hawaii Five-O* theme music. They both roared with laughter at their comic double act. But she sensed that these two were tough and effective partners out on the streets. They were both well built, assured and moved with a grace that underlined their athletic fitness. As a nurse she had many dealings with police officers as they brought into ER anything from busted jaws through to stabbing and gunshot wounds. She always got on well with them.

'Why didn't you say you were police officers?'

Chris sighed. 'These days it can be a turn-off for some people.'

She smiled, and rolled her eyes.

'Well, not for me.'

Jean looked at her watch.

'Right, you guys, I'm off to eat. Thanks for the drink; I'll take it through, if I may. There's enough here to last all evening.'

'Sure, Jean, you run along now. Catch you later.'

As she walked away she was conscious of their eyes on her back. It was always nice to be appreciated, certainly better than being ignored, but Don was the only man in her life, soon to be her husband.

But she couldn't help wondering, what if . . . ?

Would she have gone for Chris with his handsome features, curly hair and almost Tony Curtis-like looks and laughing eyes, or Steve, with his pockmarked face that added a veneer of toughness and a feeling that with him around, a girl would never be afraid of anything or anybody ever again?

But she *was* engaged to Don, so as she

entered the restaurant her thoughts immediately turned to finding a dining companion to
back up her excuse.

The last thing she wanted was to get
further involved with them.

2

Next morning, full of energy, Jean came down to an early breakfast; all worries about Chris and Steve had vanished with the new day.

The whole morning and early afternoon were hers to do what she wished, and there was only one thing on her mind.

This was the day when she would cross to Inverdee; to walk the little roads and the market square of her mother's home town.

The first boat was due to leave in three quarters of an hour, and although she could have taken a taxi, and gone the longer way round, Jean wanted, at least this first time, to arrive the old, romantic way, like her mother had talked about.

Later, mid-afternoon, they were off to Glasgow, to see the production of *Tosca* by Scottish Opera. She'd never been to an opera, and before the performance there was to be supper in a Glasgow restaurant after a bus tour of the city. Wonderful as that would have been under normal circumstances, today she was more excited by her first visit to Inverdee.

There was no sign of Kath, and despite the

early hour, Chris and Steve's table showed that they had already gone, the empty plates indicating the big breakfasts they'd consumed.

She supposed the earlier you got to the river-bank, the better.

In keeping with all the new things she was going to do, Jean decided to be adventurous, and ordered the smoked haddock.

It was delicious.

But there was no time to leisurely enjoy her meal. As soon as she was done, she was back up in her bedroom, scrubbing her teeth.

It made her think of Don, worried as to how he was getting on.

Down at the jetty she had to wait another ten minutes, watching the boat arrive. It turned out to be a small fishing craft that had been adapted to carry passengers. When it came the time to board, the women were helped down by one of the crew, a young lad who made no effort to disguise his appraisal of her as he held her effortlessly under the elbow for fractionally longer than was strictly necessary. Jean frowned to show her disapproval, knowing that really she was being hypocritical. As long as she was in control and didn't feel threatened, it was, after all, a compliment.

But as the breeze lifted her hair, blew it

across her face, her spirits rose, as did her anticipation as the little houses of Inverdee grew steadily closer.

It took ten minutes to reach the other side. When Jean finally walked up the cobbled slope and into the village proper her wildest dreams were fulfilled. The small whitewashed cottages were spick and span, with many porchways covered in honeysuckle. Window boxes and wooden tubs threw a profusion of richly coloured flowers into stark contrast with the whiteness of the walls.

As she wandered the narrow little lanes Jean began to imagine her ancestors living there: perhaps in that wee small house with the cute little door that you would need to stoop to get through, or that one with a crazily leaning chimney. Her grandparents' old address she had written down, but the sheer beauty of the place had momentarily distracted her. She turned a corner looking down at her open purse, finding her diary to get — The collision almost knocked the breath out of her as she walked into someone. She would have fallen flat on her back if it had not been for the hands that reached out and held her tightly around the waist. Jean's legs momentarily lost their capability to hold her up. Instinctively, her hands flew to the body in front of her for support. What they found was like a brick wall, albeit a supple one.

When she tilted her head back and looked up, Jean found herself gazing into piercing blue eyes, made bluer and deeper by the black hair swept straight back and tied into a short ponytail. Beneath their steady gaze her own faltered, moved to the rest of his face; first to the dark eyebrows, then to the fine aquiline nose set above a firm mouth; his blue-glazed chin had a dimple.

'Are you all right?' His voice was soft, with just a hint of the lilting accent of Kath's. Jean found her own, was surprised at its huskiness.

'Yes — yes thank you.' There was another pause, and suddenly her cheeks coloured with embarrassment as she realized she was still clinging onto him. 'Oh.' Her hands flew down to her sides. She tried to step backwards, but his hands remained firmly, but gently, around her waist.

'Are you quite sure?' His blue eyes continued to appraise her, and now she could see a twinkle in them. Despite everything, that annoyed her. He was laughing at her now.

Jean's chin came up. 'Yes, quite sure thank you. Please release me.'

For a breathtaking second he held onto her, and then she was free. For the first time she was able to take in the rest of him. He was about six foot two or three inches tall, broad shoulders covered by a military-style dark green sweater with epaulettes and leather shooting patches. He wore expensive-looking tailored riding breeches, with shining brown leather boots that reached his knees.

She found her voice, this time managing to sound firm, decisive. 'I'm sorry about that; I really wasn't looking where I was going.'

He gave a sardonic smile, which she found infuriating, and said, 'I take it that you're not from these shores — American?' He made 'American' sound somehow as if that explained everything.

She struggled to disguise her annoyance. 'How very observant of you. Yes as a matter of fact I am. I do hope I haven't hurt *you* in any way?'

His left eyebrow rose in a quizzical manner, and suddenly Jean felt her cheeks burning again at the implication that she had not intended as he continued, 'I'm in fine working order, thank you. Are you staying at the hotel?'

Jean stopped herself just in time from telling him, saying instead, 'Well, if you are okay I'll be on my way. Thank you again.' She smiled her best smile and walked on. No way was she going to let him pester her for the rest of her time here.

But as she turned the corner she shot a quick glance back in his direction, and immediately regretted it. He was still standing there, hands on his slim hips, a triumphant grin on that wildly attractive face. Jean could have kicked herself. What on earth did she think she was doing, showing him that she thought he was worth a second look? His overbearing manner more than compensated for a great figure and a face that would do justice to a movie star. No, she shouldn't kick herself; it was his tight little butt that needed the swift attention.

Jean strode on, for the moment totally forgetting what she was supposed to be doing. Her mind was in a turmoil, unable to understand why she was so upset by such a quick encounter. The man had seemed to get under her skin by just grinning at her. Never had she been so easily infuriated by anybody — *ever.*

Jean was still fuming when she reached a crossroad, but as she turned up the hill, there in front of her was a house, with a door set in the middle of two bay windows. But unlike all the rest of the village there was an air of neglect, of shabbiness in its obvious emptiness.

All of a sudden Jean experienced a

premonition, fumbled again for her diary and the address. There it was: Braemore — Shepherds Hill. She glanced up at the road name on the wall beside her. It read, Shepherds Hill. With a growing sense of unease she drew nearer the sad-looking house, and finally stood before it. Half obscured by an overgrown ivy she made out the name — Braemore. It must have been a full minute in which she just stared helplessly at the old building, before, with a metallic screech she opened the rusty gate and walked up the weed-infested path.

At the door, with difficulty, she raised the stiff, lion-shaped knocker and managed one loud bang followed by a quieter one. Nothing stirred inside; no sound of movement other than a large crow that frightened her by flying away screeching from the roof.

Plucking up her courage she moved to the windows, tried to look through their grimy exterior but to no avail, and then moved to a side gate with flaking white paint. It was totally against her nature to be so forward — brave even — considering the gloomy and somewhat eerie atmosphere. But in the event, it was immovable, and far too high to look over.

Disappointed, Jean stepped back into the road and looked up at the bedroom windows.

They stared blankly back at her. She hung around disconsolately for another ten minutes, even asking a woman who came out of the house next door if she could tell her anything about Braemore and its present owners. The woman shook her head. 'We've only been here ourselves for two months — it's definitely empty.' She gave Jean a strange, almost shifty glance, and then asked, 'Do you have a reason for being interested?'

Some sixth sense stopped Jean from telling her about it being where her grandparents had lived. Instead she made up a story about looking to buy a house. As she walked away, glancing back at the corner, she realized that she had turned up more questions than she had answers. Why, for instance, had they never visited here as a family, always her grandparents had come to them? It wasn't because of money, she was sure, because she knew that her parents had helped out in that department. Then again, she now began to realize that her mother had made a couple of trips over in recent years when she could have accompanied her, but the suggestion was never made that she should do so. And with the onset of her training as a nurse, that, and everything else of course, had gone by the wayside.

But to Jean the biggest puzzle at the

moment, was, why was Braemore empty, and so woefully neglected since her grandparents had died. Who owned it now? Jean had no recollection of her mother talking about inheriting a property. She remembered her feeling that first morning, talking to Kath, that there was a mystery about her family here, in Scotland.

Down by the village square she found a little café and went inside. It was full of copper pans on the walls, and several big old irons decorating alcoves. Although the tables were bright and clean, there was a damp, musty smell about the place. Jean ordered coffee, and stared moodily out of the window watching the world go by, a world so very different from the wide streets of Wichita Falls.

'Well, if it isn't our little visitor from the colonies!'

Startled, Jean half turned to find a tall figure standing right over her. The darkly handsome face once again had that mocking look. For a moment Jean found she could do nothing, held by those extraordinarily clear blue eyes. Then she experienced an over-whelming irritation that amazed her, given everything else about him. In normal circumstances she would have been crying out like every woman for miles around for him to speak to her. But it didn't take Germaine Greer or a rampant feminist to instinctively realize he had an attitude problem. Jean decided that attack was the best form of defence. Anyway, it would give her the opportunity to do something she really wanted to do — take another good look at him!

Slowly, with obvious deliberation, she let her gaze wander down his whole body, from the top of his raven-black hair; to his face and those blue eyes fringed by lashes a woman could only dream of, (oh why was life so unfair?); then on to his lean, firm mouth, wide, square shoulders that she already knew were as hard and as strong as they looked; the narrow waist with not an ounce of fat anywhere in sight; to the tailored breeches that covered those long limbs.

She allowed her gaze to linger *there* a fraction before slowly returning it to those devastating eyes. They were challenging her, asking, did she find everything to her satisfaction? Jean was aware of her cheeks colouring, but pressed on, putting an edge to her voice. 'You again! Are you following me around or what?'

He raised a dark eyebrow and tilted his head slightly, the light shimmering on his hair. 'Well now, I might ask you the same thing, only you see, I happen to own the place and was just checking to see if there were any problems.'

Jean winced, and said brusquely, 'Everything's fine, thank you.'

That infuriating smile didn't go away. Instead he drawled, 'Sorry, but I meant problems for the staff.'

All Jean wanted at the moment was for the floor to open up and swallow her. Her cheeks really began to burn. 'Oh . . . I-I'm sorry, I —

He suddenly held out his hand. 'I'm Adam Crawford.'

Jean lifted up her own. It was taken and held surprisingly gently in his, though she revelled in the hardness of his skin, so different from that of Don or any other man in her experience. Doctors' hands, by nature of the work, were soft, never like the one holding hers now. It seemed to her as different from her own as chalk to cheese, and it sent a shiver down her spine at the thought of it . . . Angrily, she stopped herself. What on earth was she doing, behaving like a swooning slip of a girl — and to this man in particular? Despite, in fact *especially*, because he was so dishy, and he obviously knew it, he couldn't be allowed to get away with anything he liked.

'Really? Adam? How appropriate! Did you

give rise to that old saying, 'Since Adam was in the Highlanders'?'

His mouth drew up at the corners in a sardonic smile. 'Now where did you hear that expression — not in the New World, surely?'

There he went again, making it sound as if she had come from another planet.

She smiled over-sweetly, and said, 'From my grandmother, to be exact,' and withdrew her hand.

'Really now? Your grandmother wouldn't by any chance have come from Britain would she?'

Jean felt she was getting on top at last. 'Maybe.'

The hand she had held moved to his chin and stroked it speculatively. 'Wait a minute, with that colouring you must be a Celt. She came from Bonnie Scotland, didn't she?'

Jean took a final sip of coffee and set the cup down. 'As a matter of fact, yes.' With any other person she would have been eager to have discussed her family, and the mystery of Braemore; anyone that is, but this man Adam Crawford. There was something about him — about the atmosphere that seemed to be generated between them that made it impossible for her to think or act clearly.

Jean made no further effort to explain, or say anything; she just sat there. He suddenly leaned forward, one hand on the table beside her. 'Are you staying at the hotel for a while, or just passing through?'

Before she could consider the matter properly she heard herself saying, 'For a couple of weeks.' Immediately she could have bitten her tongue out. Why oh why was she telling him what he wanted to know just like that? Then she relented a little; after all it was a pretty ordinary question.

He didn't pull away. 'So you will be around for a little while — that's good.'

It was her turn to raise an eyebrow, to which he responded with an unexpectedly warm smile, 'Perhaps we shall meet again — and soon.'

Jean looked up into those blue eyes, which seemed suddenly warmer and deeper, showing a sensitive, thoughtful person, one she could relate to more than the arrogant near-bully she had experienced before. So it was quite a surprise to hear herself reply, 'I don't think that's likely.'

Instantly, the mocking look came back. 'I wouldn't be too sure about that. Inverdee is a pretty small place.'

Jean made it obvious she was about to stand up, but he didn't immediately take his arm away.

'Excuse me, I have to go now. I'm meeting

somebody.' Jean was shocked at the totally unnecessary lie. Why was she acting in such an uncharacteristic, irrational manner?

He straightened up. 'Lucky person. Your husband, perhaps?'

Jean instinctively covered her hand.

'No — no, I'm meeting a friend.'

She stood and pulled her bag onto her shoulder, suddenly overcome with an urge to get away, which was odd since another part of her was desperate to stay.

'Excuse me.'

He moved aside, but not enough. Jean's mouth set firmly. There he went again acting like an overgrown schoolboy. She brushed past him, turned at the door. 'Goodbye.'

He lifted one long limb and placed his booted foot on her vacated seat, hand on his knee, the other on his hip, the gesture somehow proprietary, as if he was saying he not only owned the chair, but anyone who sat in it — like her. Really, he was the most infuriating man she had ever met.

'Goodbye, Miss . . . ?'

Jean chuckled. At last she could score a final parting shot. 'I didn't say.'

As she closed the door he gave her a look that said, if she belonged to him . . . He lifted the hand on his knee and brought the flat of it down with a suggestive slap on his breeches.

As Jean walked away she could feel her cheeks reddening. What was wrong with her hormones? Damn! That overbearing man had the gall to think he was God's gift to women.

But she had to admit that she was still tingling with the sensation of the nearness of him, the sweet smell of his masculinity.

For the moment she had totally forgotten Braemore.

3

As she sailed away on the little ferry, leaning over the stern, watching and listening to the raucous screams of the seagulls as they swooped over the creamy wake of the boat, she was suddenly aware of a rider galloping out of the village, climbing away up the grassy hillside. A horseman expertly handling his mount — then she caught her breath as he pulled the horse up short onto its back legs, and waved — at *her*!

Jean saw then who it was, the wild gyration of the horse throwing its rider's black ponytail into stark relief against the skyline. Adam Crawford spurred his mount on and disappeared over the hill, leaving Jean shaking her head in disbelief. Were all men always boys at heart?

Nevertheless, she had to admit to a weird feeling not a million miles from the tense excitement and dread she had felt as she had prepared to go into the operating room for the first time in her training. Exasperated with herself, she stomped off down below to get a drink.

At the hotel Jean got her keys from

reception and made her way upstairs to her room. She opened the door, intent on lying on the bed for a few minutes' rest, so she instantly saw the two dresses and a frothy half-slip draped over them together with a length of tartan material. Of course; she had momentarily forgotten the Highland Ball on the Saturday night, and Kath's promise to sort something out for her.

Jean groaned. After her morning's experiences she was beginning to wish it elsewhere. And if Chris and Steve were going . . . She held up the first full-length dress, a green satin number. Pinning it with one hand to her hip she tried a few side to side movements. It certainly did something for her, bringing out the colour of her hair, but she was unhappy with the shoulders. Disappointed, she laid it back down and picked up the other. It was only then that she saw the note from Kath and the shoes. She put the dress down and picked up the hotel notepaper and read, 'Jean, herewith a couple of dresses. I think you'll look fantastic in either, but the white is the traditional one, worn with the Sinclair Tartan sash. See you on the night, if not before — Kath.'

Jean picked up the white floaty dress and held it to her as she twirled in front of the mirror, but knowing already which one she would wear. It came down to just below her knees. The tiny heel-less dancing pumps with their old-fashioned buckles would be clearly seen. Yes, she would definitely wear it; the excitement of going in her family's tartan outweighed all other considerations, and besides, the dress and shoes had an unusual, wonderfully different feel to anything she was accustomed to wearing.

She hung the dresses in the large Victorian wardrobe, with the pumps, and then set about changing for the evening visit to Glasgow.

She chose a loose summer dress with a pashmina to put around her shoulders as she had been advised that it could get quite cold in the evenings.

Downstairs, everybody was dressed up more than she had seen before, with a great many of the ladies obviously having been to the hairdressers. Glasses of wine were being handed out. Sipping hers, Jean mingled with them, feeling slightly out of it as most of them seemed to have been to operas before.

The bus finally arrived, and the chattering, laughing crowd boarded. There was quite a party atmosphere, and as they wound their way down to Glasgow the guide distributed song sheets and they sang traditional Scottish airs including the lovely *Skye Boat Song*.

Jean had a nice voice; she had been in the school choir, and now she gazed out of the window at the passing hills, singing softly.

'Speed bonnie boat like a bird on the wing
Onward the sailors cry
Carry the lad that's born to be king
Over the sea to Skye.'

And as she sang, Jean was vaguely aware of a sensation — just like she had before — as they had left Oban; a feeling that she was not . . . *alone.*

It wasn't frightening; in fact, it was as if she was aware of somebody — but *not* a stranger, sitting beside her, with her, *in* her.

Jean knew she had a vivid imagination. When reading novels she became engrossed in the characters' lives to the point that she was completely immune to things going on around her. But as soon as she was aware of the feeling it almost as quickly evaporated, leaving her wondering if it had really happened, if she was just being silly.

Jean had never experienced anything like it before she had arrived in Scotland. Perhaps it was the tide of emotion she had brought with her, and the wonderfully evocative countryside, and Inverdee, with its past history for her family.

As the bus turned out onto a wide highway and the signs showed Glasgow was only forty miles away, Jean's thoughts turned to the visit she was going to make to Inverness. She wondered how far she would get in her quest to find out more about her mother's family.

The singing had stopped and the guide was coming down the aisle, giving out the tickets for the opera.

Jean wondered if she was going to enjoy it — was slightly resentful that it interrupted their Highland interlude. But, she conceded, it was the modern cultural life of the nation.

She took her ticket. Ah well, she could always doze, and it would be nice to see something of Glasgow.

But she didn't doze; not for a second.

As they drove home through the soft night air of summer, the bus darkened, voices hushed, Jean's mind was still full of the drama she had just lived through — *lived*, because the impact on her had been just that.

It was the most powerful, evocative music she had ever experienced.

Jean had been transfixed from the moment the curtains opened to reveal the inside of the church of Saint Andrea in Rome, and later the appearance of the hero, Mario Cavaradossi, to the final tragic scene where Tosca, maddened by his death, and about to be arrested for murder, flung herself from the battlements of a place that looked very much like Edinburgh Castle.

Puccini's music had stirred in her passions, fantasies, desires she had not had since she was a pubescent teenager. It had left her feeling utterly bereft, and full of heartache.

And *guilt*.

Because, as she climbed into bed and turned out the light in her emotionally heightened state, the image she kept seeing as the music soared in her head, was not Don, but the impossibly egotistical, hateful man she had met in Inverdee.

Adam Crawford.

Exhausted, and increasingly cross with herself, she finally fell into a troubled sleep.

★   ★   ★

Jean was quite late getting down for breakfast, a lot of the cleared tables showing that people had already had theirs.

Sleeping in late after a somewhat disturbed night had given Jean a thick head, that even a long shower had not alleviated.

A beaming Kath bustled up with a coffee pot, upturned Jean's cup and began to pour as she said, 'Good morning sleepy head.'

Jean winced.

'Morning, Kath.'

'You haven't forgotten what day it is, have you?'

For a second Jean looked perplexed, then groaned.

'Oh, you mean the ball tonight? Kath, I've got a splitting headache, I — '

Kath set the coffee pot down.

'Have you taken anything for it?'

Jean shook her head, and then regretted it.

'No, haven't got anything with me.'

Concerned, Kath asked shyly, 'Is it the time of the month?'

Even through her pain Jean couldn't help but smile.

'No, definitely not.'

Kath cheered up.

'In that case, I've got some smashing tablets — I keep a strip in my locker. I'll get you a couple for you to take with your breakfast.'

Jean started to protest but Kath was already on her way to the service exit door.

Two-handed, elbows on the table, Jean raised the cup to her lips, took a sip. As a nurse she was generally abstemious or very careful about what she took — she'd seen too many overdoses and liver damage in her time.

When Kath returned she slipped the foil strip out of her uniform pocket and pushed it under Jean's side plate, whispering, 'I don't want Mrs McPhearson to think I'm pushing drugs. Take two now, another two in four hours' time. I guarantee you'll be walking on air by the afternoon. They never fail to work for me.

'Now, what can I get you?'

When Jean had ordered and Kath was gone, she slipped out the foil, turned it over, read the composition. Apart from paracetamol it contained codeine, an addictive that was banned in some countries and available only with a doctor's prescription in others. But it was apparently sold over the counter here.

Jean would never have taken them back home, at least, not without the supervision of a doctor. She could cheat, tell Kath she'd taken them when she hadn't, but . . .

Her head throbbed, and she was on holiday and Kath was so keen for her to go that night that it would be awful to disappoint her. Jean punched out two, swallowed them quickly with some water.

By the time she'd finished breakfast her head had at least ceased to throb, felt only heavy, her forehead pinched.

As she had nothing planned, Jean decided to walk down through the extensive grounds — the fresh air would do her good.

As she strolled out onto the terrace, past

the dining room, through the window she saw Kath cleaning her table.

She waved, and mimed that her head was getting better. Kath's face beamed, and she acknowledged Jean with a little wave of her hand, hiding it with her body from the room behind her where Jean could just make out Mrs McPhearson supervising the clearing of the finished tables, and the setting up for lunch.

Jean went down the wide stone steps that led to the sweeping green lawn with a giant cedar tree in the middle. To the left she barely noticed a summerhouse set back into the bushes, its windows facing the loch. Jean could have no idea how much it was going to change her life — for ever.

She walked for quite a way, leaving the hotel grounds by a little gate, following a path that led just through a little wood of pine trees, then between gorse and heather until she reached a rocky outcrop and sat down, gazing out down the length of the loch, the waters ruffled by a slight breeze. It lifted her hair, blowing wisps across her face.

Jean breathed in the moist-filled air, tasting the salt from the sea that was beyond the nearest mountain.

Her mother must have been very much in

love with her father to leave this enchanting land.

It was then she realized her headache had completely gone.

On the way back she thought of the visit they would be making tomorrow to Inverness the capital of the Highlands. She had been told that there could well be offices there that might be of use with records and things that would help her in her quest. She meant to ask at reception, but forgot when she came across the ballroom being decorated for the evening's entertainment. She stood chatting to a couple she had met on the plane, who told her excitedly that there was haggis — *real* haggis — on the night's menu, selections of the finest single malts, whatever they were, sword dancing and, of course, bagpipes and singers.

Up in her room again, Jean kicked off her shoes and lay on the bed, then switched on her TV, but in no time at all she dozed off.

It was getting quite dark when she awoke, and she got up with a rush. But there was still plenty of time.

She slipped into a nice long, hot bath. When she had dried herself she pulled on the white towelling robe provided by the hotel, and sat at her dressing table, fixing her face. She decided against putting on pantyhose because the buckled flat-heeled pumps looked right on her bronzed legs. Also, she was wondering about the wildness of the night's dancing. Anyway it seemed natural to be bare-legged, like a country girl.

Jean finally drew on the white dress and pulled the little puff sleeves into position.

She was aware that the whiteness of the dress enhanced the honey colour of her Texas sun-kissed skin where it showed in the V-neck.

Jean slowly became aware of feeling that she was . . . ? No, she couldn't define what it was; perhaps it was just being there, in Scotland, and on her own for the first time.

She put her head through the tartan sash — the Sinclair Tartan — and arranged it so that it sat correctly on her shoulder, passed between her breasts, thankfully covering a little over-exposure of cleavage due to the new bra she was wearing, and rested correctly on her hip.

She surveyed the finished woman in the mirror. Suddenly, goose pimples rose on the back of her neck. She just looked so different from her usual self, really like another woman, from another country, from another *time* even.

She was overcome with the compulsion to alter her normal appearance. Jean began to deepen her eyes, to make them more mysterious — and then added a little more lipstick, making her lips fuller. On impulse, she tousled her hair, shook her head, so that it tumbled like flames around her face.

At last she sat back, saw a woman they had never seen in little old Wichita Falls. The grin at the thought slowly died away as the same strange sensation she'd been having over-whelmed her. But this time for a fleeting second there seemed to be another woman in the mirror but again, she *wasn't* a stranger. Jean could feel the woman breathing, drawing breath as she did, *when* she did; could feel the material of the sash where it touched her skin, the light caress of her hair on her shoulders when she moved; above all could feel the bursting excitement about what was going to happen that evening when —

As quickly and as unexpectedly as it had come the sensation dissolved away, leaving Jean looking back at what she knew was just her own reflection.

Except — the excitement was still there, coursing through her blood. She couldn't wait to get out and go downstairs. Hurriedly she put a few bits into her shoulder *bag*, puzzled for thinking of it like that and not as her purse as she would have done in the States, and made for the door.

It was strange walking in the flat-heeled pumps. They made her feel so much smaller, certainly more vulnerable, more feminine in a strangely old-fashioned way, almost like a girl again.

At the top of the stairs she paused, took in the view. It was absolutely thrilling, like a set from a Hollywood movie shooting a period piece in a Scottish castle. The place was thronging with women in dresses, their sashes displaying lots of different coloured tartans. But it was the men who looked wonderful, nearly all of them wearing dark Highland dinner jackets with silver buttons and piping on the sleeves. And, of course, they were wearing the kilt, some rather self-consciously, she noted as she made her way down the stairs. At the bottom a waitress offered her a glass from a tray. 'Champagne, madam?'

Eagerly, still taking in the scene, Jean took a glass. 'Thank you.'

'You look stunning.'

Startled, Jean looked more closely at the girl, and then suddenly saw who it was. 'Gosh I'm sorry, Kath, I didn't realize it was you.'

Kath chuckled. 'I'm not surprised, dressed like this.'

Jean took in the blue dress not too dissimilar to the green one she had rejected, but this one looked much better on her friend.

'I didn't realize you were going to be working — that's a shame.'

Kath chuckled, 'Not at all. We do the reception but we get to eat and of course then we help to organize the dancing — it's fun.'

Jean looked around, eyes shining. 'It's absolutely wonderful. I'm so grateful to you for making me come.' She held her dress and did a half twirl, 'and for the fabulous dress.'

Kath nodded, 'Talk about you not recognizing me, I had to look twice at you to be absolutely sure. You look so different — it's incredible — what have you done to yourself?'

Jean chuckled. 'I don't know, I think you're to blame.' They both laughed.

A whole crowd of Jean's fellow Americans came in, hooting with laughter and wise-cracking, and started taking glasses from Kath's tray.

Chris and Steve grabbed a glass of champagne each.

'Well, look at you. Give us a twirl.'

She did so, suddenly finding a blinding flash of light right in her face as she came around again.

Chris had produced a camera. Jean winced. 'Don't waste your time on me.'

Steve shook his head. 'Why not? You look swell — really cute.'

Somebody from the tour party came past.

'You guys, you're not dressed up.'

They started to protest but he grabbed Steve by the elbow, pointed at a corner table.

'They've got hats; get one on.'

They groaned, looked despairingly at each other but Jean chuckled.

'Go on, don't be spoilsports.'

Reluctantly they moved off to get a hat each.

She took a sip of her champagne, felt the bubbles tickling her nose. 'What's the form then, what happens?'

Kath had to wait before she answered, as another crowd took all the rest of the glasses on her tray.

'First comes the dinner, then you listen to some traditional songs performed by the people from Inverdee, then' — she held her arms above her head, including the tray, and did a little jig — 'you dance.'

Jean giggled nervously, 'But I warned you, I don't know what to do!'

'That's all right, each table's got a couple of the dancers on it. They'll show you; everybody's in the same boat.' Kath tapped the tray with a finger. 'I've got to get a refill. I'll see you at the table. I fixed it so that we would be together.'

Jean chuckled with delight. 'That's great! How did you manage that?'

Kath pulled a face. 'I don't work here for nothing, you know. We're over there, the table in the middle.'

Jean followed the direction of Kath's finger. 'Right next to the floor.'

The Scots lass chuckled. 'Only the best for the friends of Kathleen Kirk. And we're on the table of the Laird's son — he's to be your partner.'

Jean gulped. 'How the devil did you manage that?'

Kath started to push her way through the crowd in the direction of the kitchen. 'Mrs McPhearson isn't as bad as she looks, you know. Besides, you're the best looking one on the trip.'

Flattered, but worried, Jean protested, 'But I don't know anything.'

She heard Kath's reply but the latter already had her back to her. 'Don't be such a worry-boots; we're all together and in any case he's the president of the Highland Dancing Society — he'll show you what to do.'

Then the crowd closed in behind her and Jean was alone, but not for long. Soon the noisy excited throng involved her and she was in an animated conversation when suddenly a big gong in the entrance hall was struck and the hotel manager's voice came over the microphone. 'Ladies and gentlemen, will you please go to your tables and prepare to welcome your president and his party for the evening.'

Such was the rush that Jean was carried along by the throng and found herself by the table in no time. She checked the name cards by the place settings, and was glad Kath wasn't there to see her face when she discovered that sitting next to her was 'The President'.

The others on the table, she noted with relief, she already knew, completed by a breathless Kath when she arrived with a lad in tow who Jean recognized as being another member of staff.

At that moment there was a sudden wail that gathered strength and became the full-blooded roar and scream of bagpipes. The piper led the way followed by a small party of women and men; the latter all dressed in kilts. Jean was delighted to see that in the case of the women, they were wearing white dresses like hers with tartan sashes. That made her feel authentic, a bit different from her fellow hotel guests whom she joined in the regular clapping in time to the party's progress. At each table one of the party, be it a man or a woman, turned off and joined it, until as he drew nearer only the fine tall figure of the president was left with the piper.

Jean's jaw dropped. Her legs felt weak as the president stood beside her and the piper continued to play for a moment, and then ended with a flourish. When the last of the clapping had died away the manager's voice came over the microphone again. 'Ladies and gentlemen, please be silent for grace.'

Beside her the deep voice of Adam Crawford rang out.

Jean, head ostensibly bowed, took in the man beside her. He was much taller than before, until she remembered her flat-heeled pumps. She barely came to halfway up his chest with its white ruffle standing out from the dark jacket. His long, muscular legs, projecting from underneath his reddish kilt, were darkly tanned, covered in hair that was lighter than that on his head, and dived from view beneath knee-length socks turned down at their tops. From the edge of the nearest one jutted the jewel-encrusted top of his dagger that was worn on such occasions.

The grace was finished, and she found herself looking up into frowning blue eyes that seemed to be appraising her as if he had only just met her for the first time. He breathed, 'My God, is it really you?'

Jean nodded, found it difficult for a second to find her voice, and then hissed, 'It is, and you don't exactly look the same either.'

He shook his head as he held her chair for her to sit down, the small ponytail making him look like an eighteenth-century Highland chief.

'You're a different looking woman from this morning, that's for sure.'

Jean knew what he meant, felt it inside, too. And strangely, instead of being irritated by his presence, she felt that he too seemed, somehow, different.

She smoothed the dress under her and sat down.

Before he sat himself he went around the table, introducing himself and kissing the ladies' hands, including, Jean noticed, Kath's. The latter gave her a sly smile and whispered when he was out of earshot, 'Well you can't blame me, can you? Isn't he dishy?'

Finally, he sat down beside her. His leg momentarily brushing hers where her dress had ridden up — skin to skin.

He looked at her name on the card as he took his napkin and murmured, 'So it's Jean Sinclair?'

Jean swallowed self-consciously, aware that

the last time they had met she had refused to tell him.

'I'm sorry about that, it was rather childish of me.'

He chuckled and put out his hand, 'Let's start again.'

Jean placed hers into his and he gently put his other on top of it, and whispered, 'Hello again — Jean.'

She gave an impish grin. 'Hello — is it your Lairdship or just plain sir?'

He gave a throaty chuckle. 'Adam, though I asked for that the way I behaved this morning.'

Jean looked demurely down at her empty plate, and said in a whisper, 'You were rather . . . ' she paused, finding it difficult to find the right words to express what she wanted to say, ' . . . forceful about what you wanted to do to me when I left.' She was halfway through the sentence when she realized just what she was saying; what she was implying; that her cheeks were already beginning to burn. Inwardly she took herself to task, staggered that she was bringing up the humiliating memory.

He said nothing immediately, and she was forced in the end to glance at him to see if he had heard.

Her desperate hope was not to be. Jean

found herself looking into two twinkling and surprisingly warm blue eyes that looked steadily back into hers. She thought she would die waiting in suspense until he spoke; sure she was going to be unmercifully teased.

'Put it down to an inadequate man floundering about trying anything he could to impress a beautiful feminist.'

Flattered, and sensing that her embarrassment had gone undetected, had in fact been mistaken for something else but not knowing what he was talking about, Jean said, 'What do you mean?'

He chuckled, 'Oh come on, you know exactly what I mean, the way modern feminists are expressing themselves, saying that the ultimate freedom of women, the last thing for them to explore is the fantasy of wishing their men to be more physically forceful — on demand, of course. One minute you want us to be wimps, the next masterful. Isn't that so?'

Jean chuckled with relief. 'Yes of course, any woman does. Incidentally, I'm not a feminist.'

Further conversation was cut short by the arrival of the waitress who began to place a small portion of something that looked like thick mince on her plate. Temporarily obscured from his view by the girl's body she took stock of what had just happened. Was she going mad or something? What had possessed her to come out with that daft statement then and there? It was not as if she had been thinking about him in any context whatsoever, let alone like *that*! It must, she acknowledged, have been buried in her subconscious, only to explode out of her — yes that was how it had felt — when they had come into close physical contact again. As for that bit about feminists, she hadn't understood a word, except . . .

Long ago, as a girl teetering on the edge of becoming a woman, she had entertained daydreams of her 'hero' who was, of course, the captain of the college football team, having a crush on her. But in the fantasy he was always finding her doing something against school rules, and because she gave him some cheek, it often ended up with him having to order her to do some menial task. Then they kissed and made up, and later he took her to the junior prom, where he did as *he* was told as she showed him off to her green-with-envy-friends! Maybe these feminists knew a thing or two!

Jean giggled at the adolescent memory just as the waitress moved back.

'You find something amusing?' He was

grinning in puzzlement at her.

Jean shook her head. 'It's nothing, just a memory from long ago that I had quite forgotten.'

Another waitress brought two types of vegetables, and put portions by the 'mince-meat'. Jean lent forward. 'What's this then?'

He pointed with his finger over each in turn. 'That's 'neaps' — parsnips to you — and 'tatties' — they're potatoes.'

Jean began to enjoy his attention and pointed herself.

'And that's the famous haggis?'

He grinned. 'Yes, the Chieftain of the Puddin' Race, as Robbie Burns called it. There is no address to it tonight as it's not his birthday.'

She picked up her fork. 'It smells delicious. May I start?'

'Of course. Add a tiny drop of the whisky in the little jug — gives it more bite.'

Jean did as she was told, then broke off a portion and placed it between her lips, conscious that he was watching her all the time as she slowly moved it around her mouth. 'Mmm, that's delicious.'

'You like it then?' He had a teasing, expectant look.

She nodded vigorously, 'Great. What's in it?'

With great relish he enumerated, 'Sheep's heart, lungs, liver, all chopped up with oatmeal, suet and onions; the lot boiled in the stomach bag.'

Her face said it all. Jean looked at him in horror.

He picked up two tumblers already filled with a honey-coloured liquid. 'You must wash it down with a good malt.'

Hesitantly, she took one. Adam Crawford clinked his glass against hers. 'To a good evening.'

The liquid was like nothing she had ever tasted before, certainly not like what she expected of anything dispensed in small glasses. Back home tequila was a fiery drink that she had tried just once and had burnt the back of her throat. But this was nothing like that. This was soft, warming, producing a glow of well-being deep down inside.

She took another longer sip, played it around her mouth before swallowing. 'It's gorgeous, what is it?'

He gave her an exaggerated wink. 'The hard stuff. You should take it slowly, now.'

He demonstrated by eating a forkful of haggis, then taking a sip from his glass. 'That's the way to do it.'

Jean followed suit, finding the combination

superb and soon forgetting the constituents of the haggis.

She cleared her plate, and was duly greeted with a cheer by her fellow diners.

Flushed with success and feeling elated, Jean turned to Adam. 'That was marvellous!?'

'What else have you got under your kilt?' It was said without thinking, as an attempt at a joke with a Scottish flavour, but as soon as she had said it Jean realized the double meaning.

Kath put her hands to the side of her cheeks in mock horror. 'Jean, what on earth are you doing, saying that to a Scotsman?'

Another woman shrieked, 'You're asking for trouble, lassie, he might just go and decide to show you.'

They all joined in laughing. Normally, Jean would have been acutely embarrassed, but she grinned around at them, until her eyes found his. Adam was shaking his head with mock disbelief. 'Really, Jean — I think you'd better have another one of these.' He poured more of the honey-coloured liquid into her glass. When he'd recharged his own, he raised his tumbler.

'To our charming visitor to our shores. May she find out everything she wishes to know about our strange customs — and dress!'

They all roared then, but Jean didn't mind. It was only when the table had quietened down, and they had begun to talk amongst themselves again that she found herself facing those beautiful blue eyes. The dark lashes on one slowly closed and opened in a roguish wink. He didn't say anything, but Jean felt her legs go weak; was glad she was sitting down.

Fortunately they started to clear away the dishes and place new ones for the next course. A man, obviously part of the organizing committee, came and said something to Adam who placed his napkin on the table. He pushed back his chair. 'Excuse me a moment.'

As he walked away Jean stole a look at his retreating back. He really was a fine figure of a man, the kilt swaying from side to side above those strong legs. She turned back to find herself facing Kath, who was giving her an unmistakeable grin. She raised both eyebrows. 'Glad you came?'

Jean glanced quickly around the table, and was relieved to see they were all engaged in animated conversation. She hissed. 'Yes. Shh, I'll speak to you later.'

The main course was served — grouse from the local moors with a splendid selection of fresh vegetables. Adam came back and resumed his seat. 'Right, let's have some wine.'

He filled her goblet, leaning in her direction to do so. Jean could smell his aftershave as he asked, 'Are you enjoying yourself?'

'I love it!' she replied fervently.

'Do you now,' he murmured, still near her even though her glass was full. 'And what else do you love?'

Jean's eyes met his. Green melted into all-powerful blue. I could surrender everything to you, she thought. There was an alien heat in her belly that had been there since the first touch of his leg, fanned by the warmth of the malt.

'I love it here,' she whispered, her voice unexpectedly husky.

His blue eyes dropped to her lips. Slowly, softly he asked, 'Just what is it about our fair country you like the best?'

Jean ran her tongue lazily along her bottom lip to moisten it as she chose her words with as much care as her befuddled and excited mind would allow.

'I love the mountains, the lochs, the traditions, the way the men dress — like tonight.'

There was a pause, in which the word 'men' seemed to hang in the air.

Finally he sat back, grinned, 'Well now, let's hope you'll get the opportunity to see some more of those things in the next week or so.'

Jean reached for her wine, took several quick sips as Adam filled his own glass. She thanked the Lord he couldn't really read her mind.

So it came as a surprise when there was a loud roll on the gong and the manager's voice came over the loudspeaker: 'Ladies and gentlemen, will you please rise for the Loyal Toast.'

Adam helped with her chair and they all raised their glasses.

'The Queen.' The loud, commanding voice was Adam's. Startled, Jean said, 'The Queen,' in unison with everybody else, but before they sat down he said, again in a loud voice, 'And the President of the United States of America.' They all followed suit.

When they were drinking their coffee Jean said, 'Well you certainly made me jump. Are you going to do anything else unexpected?'

He grinned back at her. 'Now then, you'll just have to wait and see.'

What she would have said in reply Jean could only wonder at, because at that moment Kath, who had stood up, came and rested her hand on her shoulder.

'Shall we freshen up before the entertainment starts?'

When they were out of earshot Kath said, 'Well, you two seem to be getting on well enough!'

Jean blushed. 'He's very good company, that's all.'

Kath's look was enough. 'You're the envy of the female population, so make the most of it.'

Jean tried to shrug nonchalantly. 'When I first met him I couldn't stand the man.'

That *was* true, and it still puzzled her now.

'Has he a reputation for being, well, difficult to get on with?'

Kath held the door to the powder room and chuckled as Jean went through. 'You mean, is he a male chauvinist pig? Yes!'

They both laughed then, startling the other women. Suppressing their giggles only made it worse, and they were still chuckling when they returned to the table. To her disappointment Adam was not there, and Jean was sitting disconsolately alone when his voice whispered in her ear, 'Would you like something else to drink?'

Jean turned her head to find he was stooping down beside her, his kilt with its hairy sporran hanging between outstretched knees. The closeness of his face was, for once, lower than her own. Without thinking, Jean put her hand on his knee. 'I'll have whatever you would normally have now.' When she realized what she was doing she froze, her hand resting gently where it was, feeling the soft hair beneath.

He hesitated for a second as if he didn't want the moment to pass. Finally he said, 'I'll get us some Drambuie.'

He got up and strode off. Jean watched his tall figure, the wide shoulders leading to narrow hips, letting her gaze fall down across his swinging kilt and muscular legs. He was without doubt the most sexually attractive man she had ever set eyes on.

Jean sat back, trying to take stock of a situation that seemed to be running along of its own volition. Why, less than a couple of hours ago she had been obsessed with only one thing: the story of her family's past; of Braemore. If anybody had mentioned Adam Crawford she would have snorted with derision, remembering the wild display on the horse and his arrogant manner. But now . . . ?

'Penny for them?' It was Kath, who had come and sat in Adam's vacated chair. Jean's predicament must have looked obvious, because she didn't wait for a reply, her accent even more pronounced as she leaned closer and whispered, 'Jean, be careful. Adam

Crawford has a bit of a reputation as a womanizer; it runs in the family.'

Jean frowned. 'That's not a very nice thing to say, and in any case I should remind you it was you who sat me here in the first place, so what does that say about you?'

Kath pulled a face, held her hands up in defence. 'I was only trying to be helpful. You struck me as being well able to cope with him, after all you've travelled the world, and you being American and everything.'

Jean conveniently ignored the fact that she hadn't in fact been anywhere before and said straight out, 'You wouldn't be jealous, would you?'

It was a hurtful stupid thing to say, that would never have crossed her mind under normal circumstances. But tonight was different, *she* was different, and the circumstances were definitely not normal.

Kath sighed resignedly. 'Well, don't say I didn't warn you, okay?'

She stood up as Jean said, 'I'm a big girl; I can take care of myself thank you very much.'

'A lot of girls have said that in the past.' Kath looked at her pleadingly. 'We're still friends, aren't we?'

Jean, horrified, wondering why she had so overreacted, said, 'Of course, Kath.' The latter put her hand on Jean's shoulder and gave a little squeeze.

'Thanks.'

Jean covered it with hers and returned the gesture. 'I'm having a great time, thanks to you.'

Adam finally returned with a tray bearing a small square bottle and two tiny glasses. He set it down on the table. 'There we are, the finest Drambuie you can find anywhere in Scotland.'

He pulled out the stopper and carefully poured the thick liquid into the glasses. 'You are looking at the liqueur of the Highlands, my dear.'

Jean's heart missed a beat at the 'dear'; it sounded so intimate, so close.

He handed her a glass. 'This one you should sip.'

Jean put it to her mouth, was conscious of his eyes on her lips as they parted and let in a trickle of the viscous fluid. It was difficult to say what it tasted like. In one sense it was harsh, like cough mixture, but then, as she allowed it further into her throat, it became smooth and velvety.

Eagerly he asked, 'Well?'

'I think it's perfect.'

His face broke into a broad grin. 'That's good, because otherwise I would have to finish the bottle myself!'

They both laughed then, just as the dance floor in front of their table was filled with whooping, whirling men and pipers. They laid swords, star-shaped on the ground, points facing inwards. The voice of the master of ceremonies rang out. 'Ladies and gentlemen, the Highland Sword Dance.'

Jean watched in fascination as four men began to dance with incredible nimbleness around the blades.

'This has its origin in ancient times when it was the custom to lay defeated opponents' swords on the ground, and dance on them to show you had won.'

Jean murmured something, but really she was more aware that in leaning in to explain what was happening, Adam had put his arm around the top of her chair; she could feel his hand resting lightly on her shoulder. Without leaning forward she stretched out her arm, anxious for him not to move, yet badly needing another sip of the liqueur to steady her nerves. It seemed as if another milestone had passed; that a certain intimacy existed between them.

Jean swallowed the Drambuie, felt its warmth giving her stupid body the strength it ought to have naturally. She had always recognized and despised herself for being afraid when it came to men; not physically — although Adam would have been capable of holding her one-handed off the ground if he had wanted to — but emotionally. She couldn't stop a chuckle as she remembered Kath remarking that she had thought her some sort of tough American cookie. In relationships with the opposite sex nothing could be further from the truth.

'What's funny?' Adam's grip on her shoulder grew firmer as he leaned forward to turn his head and look quizzically at her.

Jean thought quickly. 'Oh I was wondering what the clansmen did about their defeated enemy's women — did they dance with them or on them?'

His free hand reached out, a finger playfully touching the tip of her nose. 'We Highlanders are civilized men; we always gave the ladies a choice before we let them go.'

She giggled, 'And would you give me the choice?'

His blue eyes moved around her face, finally rested on hers. Although the rest of his features were smiling, they had a serious, unwavering look.

'I think not.'

'Oh.' Jean pouted her disappointment. 'Why not?'

'Because I would never let you go again.'

Jean suddenly found it difficult to breathe, aware of her chest visibly rising and falling with the effort. This was crazy; it was all happening too fast. But the madness wouldn't be shaken off that easily.

Breathlessly she whispered, 'Wouldn't you?'

Without taking his eyes off her he slowly shook his head, 'No.'

For a split second neither of them moved, eyes locked, then Jean managed, 'You don't really know me enough to say that.'

She had nervously meant to try and make a joke of it, but it came out sounding very serious.

He didn't smile either as he said, 'I know enough, and besides, we can find out more — can't we?'

She would have said yes, of that she was not in doubt, but whether she would have qualified it in some way, like mentioning Don, or the fact she was only going to be there for a short while and she was going to be busy — all the old excuses with which she had dodged the issue when men had shown interest in the past (except for Don who had just grown on her) — she never found out because at that moment one of the whirling dancers suddenly bounced towards them as the music stopped and grabbed Adam's arm.

'Come on, sir, they all want to see you dancing.'

Adam protested, but the crowd began cheering wildly as he was dragged to his feet. Jean was thankful in one way for the breathing space, the time to try and think things through, where it was all going.

Adam gave her an apologetic look, and then kicked off his shoes. Once on the floor he took up his position, the pipes struck up, and with his arms raised above his head, began to dance as light as a feather, his stockinged feet nimbly darting between the gleaming blades. Jean watched in awe, staggered that such a big hunk of a man could be so light on his feet, then admitted that he was very athletic, not muscle-bound.

Absorbed as he was, he managed to flash her a clowning look that said, 'Help!'

Jean waved back, mouthed, 'Get on with it'. She poured another glassful, sipping it as she tried not to make it too obvious that she was fascinated by the increasing glimpses of the muscles of his thighs, the kilt flicking up higher as the music grew faster. With a sense of guilt worthy of her schoolgirl days with the nuns, she realized she was wondering if he wore anything underneath, as she had heard that it was correct for a Scotsman not to do so when wearing the kilt. Despite the fact that nobody was near her, and in any case they were all far too busy watching and screaming at the dancers, she felt her cheeks colouring — yet again — at the thought.

Fortunately or otherwise the whole thing came to an abrupt end and he staggered back and slumped into his chair. 'I'm not as fit as I used to be.'

He began to fasten his shoes, Jean helping by picking one up and preparing it as he dealt with the first.

'Where did you learn to dance like that?'

'In the Army, I was in the Queen's Own Highlanders — a short service commission. My father thought it would be a good idea for me to knock the rough spots off and get some travelling done before I settled down.'

All of a sudden Jean had to ask, needed to be reassured, 'And have you settled down? Is there someone who should be with you tonight?'

As she waited with baited breath he took the other shoe from her, the action seeming strangely domestic.

'The only person I should be with is here already.'

'Oh.' She was unable to keep the disappointment out of her voice.

He straightened up, faced her on level terms, and took both of her hands in his.

'*You*, of course, you idiot.'

Overcome by madness, she kissed him on the lips. It was over in a flash, a fleeting brush of flesh; a sensation of skin, hard with bristle; of the smell of shaving soap like her father had used; of whisky; of sweet male breath.

He raised an eyebrow, smiled gently. 'Jean, let's dance.'

It was only then she noticed that an orchestra was preparing to play. She stood, let him take her by the hand and lead her to the floor. Before he took her in his arms he pulled his sporran to one side, making her chuckle. Then she was reaching up, putting her left hand on the rock-like shoulder, the other into the gentle vice of his hand, feeling the other slide around the back of her waist, drawing her closer until their lower bodies made contact. It was the first time that she had felt the physical nearness of him as they moved in time to the slow sound of the beat, a saxophone adding its syrupy tone. To Jean it sounded like a celestial call of infinite desire. She wanted this man — physically — with an urge that frightened her to the point of weakness.

He seemed to sense it, his hand around her waist almost holding her up. They didn't speak; there was no need for that. Jean laid her head against his broad chest. She seemed to fit into him like a piece of a jigsaw, had trouble believing this was really happening to her. Her head was telling her this was stupid, not what she wanted, but her heart was thumping madly, overriding any constraint. The whole evening was like a dream. She had never believed something like this happened to ordinary girls like herself. Her heart swooped with joy.

She had no idea how long they stayed close, her eyes shut, the music mingling in her head with all sorts of wild thoughts, until suddenly reality returned as the music stopped with a drum roll and the compere's voice broke into her reverie.

'Ladies and gentlemen, please make up groups of ten for the country dancing.'

At any other time Jean would have been delighted, but not now, not with the mood she was in. They broke apart, but she was pleased that he continued to hold onto her hand. He looked carefully at her, and said softly, 'Do you want to do this, or shall we take a rest?'

Pleased, but worried, Jean waved a hand in the general direction of their table. 'Won't the others miss us? You are here to lead the Highland dancing, aren't you?'

He shook his head, 'There are others — don't you worry.'

He walked her through the crowd in the direction of the open French windows. 'Wait for me on the terrace; I'll get our drinks.'

Jean stepped out onto the flagstones; surprised the evening was so warm, the air still, not a whisper from the leaves in the tall trees. The scent of the roses hung heavy about her; the moon was so bright it was casting shadows. She walked to the stone balustrade, leant on it as she gazed across the valley, at the darker hills surrounding the liquid silver that was the loch. It was as if her senses had become enormously powerful, magnifying everything around her, like the vividness you got sometimes in a nightmare: only this was definitely no nightmare.

As the first sounds of a different, traditional Scottish music drifted out to her, Adam appeared carrying the bottle of Drambuie in one hand and their two glasses in the other.

He slowed as he approached her, stopped altogether.

Jean, who had turned and was leaning back on her hands, asked anxiously, 'Adam, what's the matter?'

He came beside her and set the bottle and glasses down on the balustrade. 'Nothing's the matter only — '

Jean put her head on one side. 'Only what?'

He filled the glasses, the moonlight strong

enough to see the levels of the now black-looking liquid.

'You reminded me of someone.'

'Oh.'

The disappointment must have registered, as he explained quickly, 'No, not a long lost lover or anything like that.' He paused then said, 'Promise you won't laugh or be offended?'

She nodded, wondering what was coming.

'Well, it's just that for a second there, what with your long hair and that dress, and the classic stonework behind, you reminded me of an old photograph I've just found.'

Jean smiled and took the glass he held out. 'As long as the woman wasn't old, there's no problem.'

'On the contrary, she was, *is*, very beautiful.'

He reached out, slowly ran the back of his fingers down the length of her hair.

Jean moved nearer and before she realized what was happening she was in his arms, the glasses shattering on the flagstones at their feet.

His mouth was firm, hard, insistent, would have brooked no resistance, not that she gave any except a token gesture before her lips parted. After his tongue entered her mouth, it changed, moving gently, exploring every part of the inside. To Jean it was fundamental carnal invasion, sending her body into an uncontrollable surge of alien desire. Never in all of her life had she experienced a kiss like this man was giving her, where she was as much a victim as a willing partner to the violation.

Jean's hands reached up from his rock-like shoulders to the back of his head, began to run through the rich thickness of his hair, finding the ponytail.

He pulled her even closer so that she could feel the thumping of his heart, the urgency of his maleness.

Suddenly he pulled away, managed breathlessly to say, 'Jean, I — ' He searched her face, unable to go on.

She knew what he wanted, desired it herself with a force that could not be denied. She placed a finger to his lips to stop him going on. 'Where?'

He kissed her finger, took her hand away and held it firmly as he led her to some steps down into the garden. As she followed him, Jean felt as if she was in one of her frequent dreams, teetering on the edge of an enormous precipice, experiencing a tremendous fear at what was about to happen but knowing that it was inevitable, and there was no way back.

She followed him in silence until he turned down a little-used narrow path. 'Where are you taking me?'

He stopped, pulled her to him, both hands on her waist, lifting her up onto the tips of her toes, as she once again reached her hands around the back of his neck. This time the kiss was gentle, his tongue only nestling against the corners of her mouth. He broke away, even though she wanted more.

'Jean, I wanted you the moment I set eyes on you.' He put his arm around her and they walked on, coming to a summer-house.

His voice was hesitant. 'This place has many happy childhood memories for me.'

They stood for a moment, and then Jean moved to the door, opened it and stood in the entrance. She held out her hand.

Relieved, he joined her, led the way unerringly in the darkness until they came to a pool of moonlight. He stopped, faced her. She knew the time had come, that they were in the eye of the emotional and physical storm that was about to engulf her — to engulf them both.

Jean's breath ceased in her thumping chest as he carefully lifted off the sash and tossed it into the darkness. She ran her tongue over swollen lips that ached again for the touch of his, but stood obediently still as he drew down over her shoulders the thin sleeves of her dress, and then undid the bodice. The light material fell to the floor around her ankles, leaving Jean suddenly exposed to air that appeared to tingle with electricity. Revealed in the flimsy bra, her breasts shone like alabaster in the moonlight. She heard him catch his breath, then as his hand came up and started to caress her flesh, he whispered, 'Darling, my beautiful, beautiful darling.'

Under his touch she felt her own hardening response, and when he bent forward and began to lightly kiss the hollow between them, she flung her head back, gasped, 'Take it off.'

As it followed the sash into the darkness of the night, another darker frenzy gripped her as she felt his tongue circling one raised nub of nipple, his hand cupping each swollen breast in turn.

Driven by forces older than mankind she pulled away his jacket, hearing its weight hit the floor, uncaring as she clawed at the buttons of his shirt until he too was bare.

His large hands seized her then, one at the back of her neck, the other between her shoulder blades, pulling her in close, so that her nipples pressed against the hairs on his unyielding, flat chest. It was the rawest sexual sensation that she had ever experienced and it blew her mind completely.

He was raining kisses on her now, light touches of his lips to her neck, ears and hair. It stopped suddenly as he groaned and broke free, tearing away the remnant of his shirt, kicking off his shoes. He never took his eyes off her as he undid the chain of his sporran and threw it aside, and then started on the buckle at his waist. She watched as he unwound the tartan cloth, caught her breath as his masculine body in all its magnificent arousal was laid bare, his skin gleaming with a surreal glow in the light of the moon, the black hair on his chest leading down to the thickness below and his aroused manhood, his limbs all sinewy strength. He suddenly reached behind him and pulled his hair free, the dark mass falling down around his shoulders. Never in her wildest fantasies had Jean imagined anything so full of raw, primeval savagery, and above all — male beauty.

She felt her own weakness and strength; weakness of body, for this man could do what he willed with her by sheer physical strength, and yet in a more subtle way, knew that it was her femaleness that was driving him into a state bordering on madness, a madness from which she could ultimately derive full control over him.

All this flashed through her mind as she put her hands into the waistband of the flouncy half-slip and pushed it down over her hips. It fell to the floor leaving her in only tiny lace panties.

He held out his hands and she went eagerly to him. With one easy sweep he lifted her off her feet and laid her gently down onto the discarded kilt. Tenderly he said her name over and over again, trailing kisses across her neck, shoulders, breasts and on to her belly, right down to the skein of silk that drove her into a frenzy of desire. She seized his glorious head of hair and forced him lower, her body jerking in an uncontrollable surge of joy. Finally he pulled away, hooked his fingers into the panties and slid them off, leaving her naked before his searching gaze.

There was a wondrous fire in his eyes as he looked at her from head to toe, an appraisal that she enjoyed to the full before extending her arms up to him in an invitation to take what was rightly his; to finally finish what he had started, and put her aching body out of its terrible, wonderful, glorious misery.

He lifted a hand, traced it gently down the side of her face until it rested at the corner of her mouth.

'Are you quite sure about this, Jean?' She knew then, if she hadn't before, that she wanted this man like no other before in her entire life. As much as he wanted her so badly, she sensed that with one word of protest from her, he would have pulled back, of that there was no doubt.

He waited for her answer, which she eagerly gave, reaching up to enclose his hand and draw it to her aroused breast.

'I want you to have everything.'

She hardly recognized her own voice, it sounded so low, the blood pounding in her head with the effect of what he had been doing to her.

Although she had never been to bed with any man before, Jean seemed to know what to do with an instinct that would later amaze her, and secretly make her blush at the memory.

He did what he wanted with her, his hand slowly stroking her inner thigh; she responding instinctively, with movements that she had no prior knowledge of, exploring the sheer perfection of his naked male body with a rhythmic abandonment that came from some inner force over which she had no control. Together they reached a point from which there was no turning back, where there was no thought in her head but that she was to become part of his flesh.

The moment of his total possession, the thrusting entry into her offered body was accompanied by a fleeting stab of pain that in itself was right; the last gesture of her former incomplete self; the rupture of the chrysalis as the butterfly broke free.

She had forgotten, totally, that she was — *had* been — a virgin. She heard him exclaim something incomprehensible as she hung on to his heaving back, clawing at his skin with her nails, crying and groaning in ecstasy as his movements reached a frenzy. A feeling of tremendous fullness engulfed her. Suddenly he gave one last, almost desperate jerk and then froze, holding her still, his head held back, roaring at the heavens as he delivered into her the genetic message as old as Man himself.

A second passed, then he groaned, withdrawing completely and collapsing alongside her.

In the sudden silence, the only sound was their ragged breathing.

Finally, Jean turned to him, cradling his head, stroking the damp lengths of hair from his face. It was the moment instinct had told her would come; the moment when his intrinsically male, physical dominance was gone and her more resilient female strength

94

came into play. She looked down at his manhood, no longer the strutting master, now lying asleep, as vulnerable as a little boy. Jean smiled; tenderly kissed his forehead, mothering the man who seconds ago had ridden her to the gates of heaven — and beyond.

There was silence for a long time before he spoke, voice different again, strangely subdued.

'Jean, why didn't you tell me?'

She knew what he meant.

'That — ' she swallowed with difficulty — 'it was my first time with anybody?'

Her heart sank at the resentment in his voice as he nodded and said, 'Yes, except I'm not anybody.'

She squeezed his arm, placed the other around to the back of his head and kissed him tenderly on the forehead.

'Of course you're not, darling. Why are you acting like this?'

Even before she saw his face, heard the anger in his voice, she knew from the way his shoulders tensed that something was terribly wrong.

'Because I would never have done it, *never*, not if I had known.'

Jean suddenly felt fear, knew that this was not supposed to be happening, not now, not after such a wonderful time together.

She pleaded, 'What was I supposed to have done — shouted it from the rooftops — signed 'virgin' after my name in the reception book?'

Abruptly, he sat up, pushing her away as he stood and began hurriedly dressing.

Hurt and bewildered, Jean curled herself into a ball, covering herself in sudden modesty. She felt the tears coming into her eyes, fought them back, determined that he should not see them. She managed, 'Adam, please don't leave me like this, please, I don't understand.'

He abruptly stopped tucking in his shirt. The furious look in his eyes made her recoil in horror.

'What were you thinking of? What a stupid, stupid waste.'

Jean's voice was on the point of breaking. 'I'm sorry. I thought — I . . . ' Despite everything the tears began to show. Miserably she wiped her hand quickly across her wet cheeks. 'Didn't you enjoy it?'

It was a mistake, she realized, as he poured scorn onto her head.

'Oh I had a great time. Nothing like a good wrestle in the sack after dinner. What is it with you? Don't you care about yourself?'

For the first time Jean began to feel

something more than just wretchedness: resentment. Her chin came up. 'If you felt so guilty why didn't you stop?'

'Because by then it was impossible.'

There was a bitterness in his voice that made her shiver. But there was also something else that gave her a glimmer of satisfaction, a sense of triumph. So the first man who had tasted the fruit that was Jean, body and soul, had been as helpless as she, swept along by an irresistible force of nature, a force that had been borne out of his desire for her. She attempted a matter-of-fact bravado. 'One thing's for sure, you don't need to worry about catching anything, do you?'

He paused then, as if he saw for the first time the tear-stained girl at his feet and took pity.

Softly he said, 'It shouldn't have happened here,' he waved his hand around at the moonlit summerhouse. 'It should have been special.'

Jean wanted to scream out that it *had* been; was the most wonderful, the most special thing that had happened to her in her whole life. But it wouldn't come. Some sixth sense warned her that if it hadn't been like that for him, she was wasting her time.

She bit back the tears as he continued, 'I would have been more . . . careful.'

There was an embarrassed silence in which Jean found it impossible to say that in that case she was pleased he had not known.

But mention of it was enough to galvanize her into action. No way was she going to lie there and listen to him denigrating what had been the most spellbinding moment in her life. It was not to be further spoilt — tarnished — more than was already happening.

She stood up, joining him as they dressed in painful silence.

Finally they were ready to leave. He went to take her by the elbow, but she shrugged him off. It was so unreal, acting as though he was a complete stranger, yet he was the one man in the world who knew her intimately.

They didn't speak as they made their way back to the terrace. At the top of the steps he paused, turned hesitantly towards her.

Even then she still longed for him to suddenly take her in his arms, say it was all a mistake. But it was not to be. In fact, it was worse.

It was the tone in his voice that finally upset her the most, a combination of indifference and coldness.

'Would you like to go back inside?'

It sounded like he couldn't have cared less what her answer was going to be.

Some vestige of pride came to her rescue. 'Thank you, but no.'

After what had gone before, she felt only a strange iciness now; knew that for her there would be much pain later — that she was still anaesthetized, still in shock.

He looked down at his feet and then up at her. His blue eyes, caught in the light coming through the French windows, were troubled. For the first time came some indication that behind his controlled exterior, inside he was not as calm as he would have her believe. He tried to take her by the arm again.

'Jean, I — '

So it was 'Jean' once more, said very softly and with warmth. It was the final straw.

She wrenched herself free. 'Forget it. I've had a great night — thank you *very* much.'

With that she walked swiftly away, holding back her sobs until she was out of earshot.

But all the way up the grand staircase they began to break through, and by the time she managed to open her door and fling herself face down on her bed she was crying uncontrollably.

What had been the most important, the most wonderful night in her life had turned into a nightmare.

Her mind raced in agony over every detail as she tried desperately to understand why he had so coldly turned against her, made all the worse by the tenderness of just moments before.

She sobbed herself into the night, the far-off sound of bagpipes finally merging with her restless, agonized sleep — a sleep in which she longed to go home to all the people who knew her, and loved her.

He would never find her again — *ever*.

4

But in the cold light of day, Jean began to feel resentment again, which finally grew into a slow, burning anger. She had done nothing wrong. On the contrary, it was he, Adam Crawford, who had the problem, although she couldn't quite figure out what that was. As she climbed off the bed and swayed onto her feet, her head felt as if she had been hit with a baseball bat. It was becoming something of a pattern.

She groaned as she looked at her reflection in the bathroom mirror. Her face was a mess, her make-up all over the place thanks to her tears, and the effects of the alcohol. She hadn't realized just how much she had consumed until now. A sudden queasiness sent her lurching to the lavatory bowl.

Later, having had an Alka-Seltzer and standing listlessly under a hot shower for twenty minutes, she started to feel she was again back in the land of the living.

But her body wouldn't let her forget what had happened.

It was only then that she thought of Don and what she had done, and with a complete stranger at that. But the expected guilt never materialized. It had been, and *was* the most wonderful thing in her life. Even the awful aftermath could not tarnish that earlier moment in time, a moment when she and Adam had become one person, not only in flesh, but something she had never been prepared for — the fusion of minds that came with it. Even though she now hated Adam Crawford, there would, she knew, be an involuntary heartache — a memory of him, and their time together, that would never be erased from her mind as long as she lived. It was, after all, her first time with any man. The memory would be hers to cherish and nobody could take that away from her — not even him.

Downstairs in the ballroom, the aftermath of the night's revelry was still in evidence. For a second she paused and looked across at their table, still littered with bits and pieces, and at the chair he had sat in. A lump came to her throat. It was truly incredible what had happened, and so swiftly, and yet she still felt no guilt, not to herself, nor strangely, to Don. That puzzled her as she made her way into the dining room. Shouldn't she have been racked with remorse?

She had barely sat down when Kath bustled up looking excited.

'Jean, how did you get on last night?'

Jean looked into the expectant face of her friend, and hesitated, before replying, 'What did Adam say when he came back to the table?'

Kath frowned. 'What do you mean?'

Jean shrugged, 'After we had been on the terrace.'

Despite her best efforts her voice betrayed the tension she felt at hearing how he had behaved, his explanation for her rather abrupt departure.

'Oh, only that you had got a migraine and had gone to bed.'

It was obvious from Kath's tone of voice and the twinkle in her eye that she at least had not believed that was the whole story.

But there was something Jean had to know. As nonchalantly as possible while pretending to scan the breakfast card, she asked, 'Did he stay much longer after I left?'

Kath made a tutting noise of mock irritation, as if to say, what did she take her for? 'Of course not, silly.' She gave Jean a sly look and added, 'He seemed to be very preoccupied and concerned.' She ran her tongue mischievously across her lower lip and added, 'Perhaps that's why he had a huge scotch and then left his car here all night.'

There was obviously no doubt in Kath's

mind why Adam had left his car: she thought he had stayed the night with her, in her room.

Jean felt her cheeks reddening at the thought that they were all talking about her, and for the first time she worried that somehow, via the others in the party from back home, Don might get to hear about it. They could be joking out loud, for example, when they arrived back at the airport and said their farewells to each other, like holiday groups do, and let something slip.

Rather abruptly she said, 'Well he certainly didn't stay with me in my room.'

It wasn't a lie, but it wasn't all the truth either, as she well knew.

Kath gave her an old-fashioned, reproachful look, but Jean carried on as if unaware that they were talking about anything of significance. 'I'll just have some toast and coffee. I'm not very hungry after last night.'

As soon as she said it she realized she should have continued with something to the effect that it was because of the excessive amount of alcohol they had all drunk. As it was, 'after last night' hung portentously in the air, but Kath chose not to make anything of it and merely said a little coolly, 'I'll get that straight away,' and turned to go.

Jean felt a rush of guilt; after all Kath was a good friend, one who could be trusted. She caught her arm. 'Kath, I'll talk to you later, when I've had more time to think.'

Kath nodded. 'Only if you really want to.'

Relieved, Jean smiled wanly up at her and bit her lip. 'I do. I've got myself into a situation and I don't honestly know what's happening.' She dropped her eyes to her hands, twisting her handkerchief in her lap. 'Why it even happened in the first place, for that matter.'

All of a sudden Kath realized that Jean was close to tears. Quickly she put her arm around her shoulders and gave her a hug. 'Anything I can do, don't hesitate to ask. I'm free in about an hour if that's any good?'

Jean got control of herself, for the first time beginning to realize just how deeply disturbed and unsettled she was.

She shook her head. 'Thank you, Kath, but I'm going on the trip to Inverness. There's something there to do with my family's past that I've been looking forward very much to following up, and in any case it will give me time to settle my own thoughts. I really don't know what to think at the moment.'

Mrs McPhearson came into view so Kath withdrew her arm from Jean's shoulders. 'I'll be around all day. When you want me, ask for this extension.' She scribbled a number on her order pad and placed it under the side plate. 'And Jean, cheer up. Whatever it is, I'm sure it will all resolve itself in the end.'

Despite the confident smile she gave her, Jean felt that Kath knew as well as anyone that that did not always follow, at least to a satisfactory conclusion. Life had a habit of not being fair!

She looked around. There was no sign of Chris or Steve, and Jean wondered if they had 'pulled', though she couldn't remember them dancing, or even dressing up properly, apart from wearing the Glengarrys they'd been given.

They had certainly been drinking, and had watched her dining and dancing, in fact had taken a lot of photographs of the occasion. Embarrassed at the thought, she wondered if they had seen her leave with Adam Crawford, had noticed their absence for such a long period of time.

After breakfast, spruced up for the journey to Inverness, she asked one of her fellow tourists when they were waiting to board the bus, if she had seen them. The answer left Jean feeling disappointed.

'Oh, the anglers? I saw them checking out very early. I was about to set out on my morning jog.'

Incredulously, Jean said, 'Checking out? I

thought they were with us for the whole time?'

The woman shrugged.

'Maybe they'll rejoin us. All they said was the fish weren't biting around here. Maybe they've gone to find other rivers — or gone home.'

If that was true, Jean was sad. She thought they would have said goodbye.

It was irrational, she knew, but she couldn't help but wonder if in any way her behaviour had led to them being upset with her.

Jean climbed up into the bus, and got herself a window seat.

That was a daft thought, she knew, just another facet of her underlying guilt.

★ ★ ★

The bus passed through some of the most beautiful Highland scenery, so different from that part of Texas she came from where you could almost see the curve of the earth it was so featureless.

Despite, or perhaps because of her emotional state, she was overcome by the soaring grandeur of the mountains. The ribbons of water cascading down them made it seem as if they were shedding tears for her.

The 'tears' fell into the mirror-like lochs

lying at their feet, formed when the glaciers of the Ice Age had retreated from the mountains, themselves thrown up by the fiery, volcanic convulsions when the very earth itself had been born.

Jean smiled wanly at her reflection in the window. The metaphor with herself, physically as well as mentally after last night, when she had gone through a similar process, was not lost on her. The Jean Sinclair she had been had ceased to exist.

The guide's voice came over the microphone. 'On your left, ladies and gentlemen, is the ruined castle of Mell. It was razed to the ground in 1493 in one of the clan wars.'

Jean allowed her gaze to fall upon the pile of stones that stuck up like a crooked finger pointing accusingly at the heavens. Was that perhaps the reason why Adam acted so weirdly with her last night? Were these Highlanders just built like that — one minute all sweetness and light, and *love*; the next minute at your throat? Back home they just called his sort plain mean-and-moody.

For the hundredth time she shook her head in bewilderment at the memory of what had happened, and particularly at his strange behaviour after what she instinctively *knew* had been something just as special for him as it had been momentous for her.

She was still brooding on things as they came down to the shores of Loch Ness. Of course, they were treated to a running commentary on 'Nessie' and the places where she had been sighted. Just for a few moments it took her mind off her own troubles as she stared at the dark, murky water and gave a little involuntary shiver at the thought of the prehistoric monster lurking beneath.

Finally they crossed the suspension bridge and entered the town of Inverness.

While the others went off sightseeing and shopping, Jean, with the help of directions from the guide, found the records office attached to the castle and museum.

Soon she was deep into local history helped by a very enthusiastic young girl who was doing a project as part of a University of Glasgow degree.

Jean explained her background.

'Can you help me find out anything about my family on my mother's side? They were Johnsons from Inverdee.'

The girl finished scribbling some more notes and then indicated a coffee machine.

'Help yourself to a cup. I'll feed these into the computer and see what it comes up with.'

* * *

Jean barely made the bus back to Inverdee. She had sat for a long time on the river-bank, watching the bubbling Ness flow out to the Moray Firth, feeling utterly devastated by what she had learnt.

Now, as the coach creaked and groaned and weaved its way back to Inverdee, she could only stare at the back of the seat in front of her. At first she had trembled with the cold, from sitting too long, but now, warm again, she still shook spasmodically, not because of a physical reason, but an emotional one . . .

* * *

The young student had bustled back to Jean, her face behind large glasses that flashed in the overhead lighting, beaming with excitement.

'This is really interesting. I wonder, would you mind if I used some of the material as part of my thesis?'

Jean felt her chest tighten with anticipation.

'No, of course not. But what is it?'

The girl sat down beside her and tapped her hand on a sheaf of papers encased in covers.

'Well, in these really old documents, there are the details of a land dispute going back centuries — grazing rights to be exact — but it all came to a head in the 1930s, and this really brings it to life.'

She opened a larger folder, and held it between them on their laps. Jean saw it was a page from the *Inverness Times* dated October 1935.

'There.' The girl pointed to a prominent feature.

'A Latter-day Highland Clearance?'

The young girl earnestly pushed her spectacles at the bridge as she rattled on about her university project, but Jean's eyes ran hungrily over the rather old-fashioned print, the names leaping out at her.

The Laird of Inverdee, one Angus *Crawford* had been in dispute with one of the locals about some sort of grazing right. He had used force to evict the family from one of his crofts. Men from the village had helped, since they were all directly or indirectly in his employ or pay.

Jean found the indignation crushing like an iron band in her chest as she read on.

The man had physically fought the Laird, no effete absentee landowner but a descendant himself of a clan chief, with bare knuckles and stripped to the waist. Up and down the street they fought, with the village folk watching until, on their knees, utterly exhausted, they had clung to each other, still aiming blows ... outside a house called *Braemore*.

There had been a court case, and the Bailie had ruled that Crawford had acted legally but that he had to provide a roof of some sort over the man and his family — a wife and a little *girl*.

In a cynical act, Angus Crawford had made available a house with no grazing rights, in fact the house outside of where the fight had finished, thus fulfilling the letter of the law, if not the spirit.

The other man had been sent to prison for a month, with hard labour, for assault occasioning actual bodily harm.

The man was Malcolm Johnson, his little daughter, Fiona Johnson was ...

Jean's *grandmother*!

Her family had been wronged and sent into a life of cold hostility, misery and poverty by the great-grandfather of Adam Crawford.

And she had ...

The thought of what had happened the night before made her legs weak, while the pressure of blood in her face was so strong that it felt as if her skin might burst.

The *shame*.

She felt wretched. An old-fashioned term she would never have thought of, would have laughed at a day ago, now exploded in her mind as the full extent of the outrage took hold of her senses.

Deflowered. She had been deprived of her virginity, used and cast aside by a man who was the grandson of the Laird.

There could be no doubt in Jean's mind that he *knew* what he had been doing, must have known somehow who she was. It explained why he was so surly with her afterwards: he couldn't wait to tell his cronies what he had done.

Even now Adam Crawford must be laughing his socks off, bragging no doubt to all and sundry about what he had achieved. He had deliberately set out to complete his family's triumph — it was in these clans-people's blood.

The shame, the humiliation was intense.

On the slow bus ride back to the hotel Jean huddled utterly dejected in her seat as it slowly dawned on her that there was only one thing she could do.

She would just pack her bags and leave, straight away that night.

She would take a taxi; expensive as that was going to be, all the way down to Glasgow and board the first flight back to the States.

Despite all her longing to see the country and the excitement of going on vacation, she couldn't bear to stay a moment longer in Scotland.

Maybe one day she might persuade Don to visit there, and not Hawaii, as they'd planned for their honeymoon, though she doubted that.

But her bitterness meant that she would never return to Inverdee.

One thing was for sure: she never wanted to see Adam Crawford again as long as she lived.

5

Back at the hotel Jean was first off the bus. Feeling tired and dishevelled she decided to have a hot bath before she packed and set off. She knew that there was a flight to the States in the morning from Glasgow, so another hour would make no real difference. What a catastrophic end to her holiday.

She asked for her key at reception. The girl turned to get it, and then as she handed it to her said, 'There's a letter for you.'

Startled, Jean took the envelope, noticed the bold, masculine strokes of her name sprawled in black ink across it, and the fact that it was without a stamp. Instantly she knew who it must be from. There was only one man who would write to her locally.

She mumbled her thanks to the girl and made for the stairs, conscious that the two receptionists were looking at her retreating back.

Deliberately, despite the fact that she had an overwhelming urge to open it there and then, see what he wanted — gloating in some way, presumably — and then tear it up with a flourish so all would see, her shaking hand tucked it into her pocket.

As she turned the corner at the top of the stairs, onto the landing, she cast a surreptitious look back. The girls were indeed looking up in her direction, then at each other with what seemed knowing glances.

Mercifully her burning cheeks were hidden from view as she continued on up out of sight.

Jean fumbled with her key, got the door open. It slammed shut as she leant back on it.

She took a few calming breaths before taking out the envelope and examining it. What could he want? What excuse was there for writing to her? She tore it open, pulled out the one folded sheet.

To begin with her eyes read the words but her brain refused to accept the meaning.

'*Dear Jean,*

What can I say about the way I behaved last night? You must think I'm completely mad, or callous, or just a plain, unthinking oaf.

The truth of the matter was — IS — that I think I have fallen in love with you, and would have wished with all my heart that we could have met in some other manner. If I had known more about you . . .'

116

He seemed to lose his way. The writing when it resumed was smaller, the ink a different colour, as if some time had passed before he had concluded,

'. . . it would, *SHOULD*, have been *SO different*. Believe me I was absolutely thrown by the enormity of what I — we — had done together.

I know I don't deserve it, have behaved badly, but I beg you — may we please start again?

If you agree, I'll be in the bar of your hotel at seven o'clock tonight, and every night this week or you can phone me.

Adam.'

There was no final declaration of love, or plea, or apology — just 'Adam'.

Her eyes flicked up to the top of the page, at the address and phone number, and then she looked at her watch. It was 6.20 p.m.

She saw through the letter and the half-hearted declaration of love straight away. What sort of a fool did he take her for? She felt the anger rising in her.

So, he wanted to humiliate her further, be seen to have her wrapped around his little finger, with all of them watching as he seduced her again, this time with the silly naive American girl actually knowing what he was like, foolishly throwing herself at him.

She snorted with anger. *'Thought'* he loved her indeed!

Jean crossed the room and started to fling off her clothes, entering the bathroom and running the taps, all the time fuming and raging.

Well, this little American girl would be in a taxi well on the way to Glasgow while he was lounging at the bar — the lizard.

Her thoughts turned to how she could add insult to his injury at being stood up in front of them all.

The embrace of the hot soapy water paradoxically began to cool the inner heat of fury, but not the desire for revenge — for the honour of her family as much as for herself.

The plan slowly took shape as she soaped herself, became firmer in her mind as she dried and powdered with extra attention.

In front of the dressing table she contemplated her face, and began meticulously to prepare herself for the coming trap, accentuating her cheekbones and using a darker shade of lipstick that made her lips look as enticing a place for a man as a Venus fly-trap was to an insect.

Mentally, she chuckled at the analogy, but not a trace of humour was allowed onto the face as she added a tiny bit more shadow to her eyes than normal — the final allure.

Jean selected a little black dress and again, because of nervous tension, felt inner amusement at the thought she was preparing herself like the black widow spider that ate its mate when he had outlived his usefulness.

And that's just what she had, metaphorically speaking, in mind for him!

Everything else she unceremoniously flung into her luggage, and then hid it behind the sofa. Satisfied, she returned to the black dress. She smoothed the figure-hugging material over her contours, checked herself front, back and sides until she was sure everything was just right.

The finishing touch took several seconds, almost a full minute, as she played with the two buttons at her cleavage, not sure if she would overdo it and perhaps give the game away.

Then, with sudden decision, she undid the buttons.

Men, even the most devious, were still easy meat — prisoners to their own macho vanity.

She was, she decided, learning fast, aided by a primitive instinct that she had never used before. Perhaps it had only been aroused by what had happened to her the previous night.

Just before she left she sprayed a rather

obvious scent around her neck and the now 'delicious' cleavage, and onto her wrists.

She checked the time: 7.26 p.m. Excellent. She opened the door. At the top of the stairs she composed herself, got into the part. Demurely, sadly, she descended to the lobby.

Even so, despite all her rage, her anger, her desire for revenge, when she saw him sitting on the bar stool, one casually outstretched leg encased in cord, a Gucci loafer resting casually on the brass foot rail, she couldn't help but feel her heart cramp in her chest.

Jean moved quietly over to him and said softly, almost meekly, 'Adam?'

Startled, he turned, stood up and looked down at her. Uncharacteristically his voice was uncertain, hesitant even.

'Jean . . . I . . . wasn't sure you'd come.'

She found herself gazing up into those beautiful blue eyes, and felt her resolve falter. It wasn't going to be easy. Adam Crawford was a man that any girl would be physically attracted to — even overawed by.

And to her he was *very* special.

He was the first man she had fully known, had become one in flesh with.

She gave a weak, quick smile, acting the part she had planned. 'To be frank, I wasn't either.'

There was an awkward pause that, finally, he broke.

'You look stunning.'

'Thank you.'

'Can I get you a drink?'

Jean thought quickly. She needed a little help with her nerves, but also needed to keep a clear head — for later.

'I'll have a spritzer.'

He turned and ordered, then faced her again.

'Shall we sit over there?'

He pointed to a corner table, and followed her as she walked ahead. Jean was conscious of the tightness of the dress across her bottom, and hoped it wasn't overdone.

They reached the table, an attentive Adam easing her into a seat.

He sat opposite, and swallowed.

'I guess I've got some explaining to do.'

Jean nodded, but said nothing. It was up to him to stew in his own juices.

He looked awkwardly into his drink, as if trying to find help there. Eventually he said,

'Jean, I admit I've enjoyed life to the full, but always with what I hoped were equal partners. And American girls are normally so . . . well, for want of a better word . . . *advanced* in their outlook.

His teeth chewed his lower lip. 'So it came

as a shock to find . . .'

She felt her cheeks colouring, and despite every effort to keep cool felt her anger rising. There was, unfortunately, a further pause as the waiter brought her drink.

When he had gone she meant to say, ' . . . You were the first?' but the words that actually came out were harsher, betraying her bitterness.

'That I was a virgin?'

It was as if she had slapped him in the face, physically turning it to one side.

But was that the case? She was aware of the direction of his gaze towards the reception area, at the girls there and the group of locals sitting by the archway.

As if to confirm her suspicion, he continued looking that way for a moment, before facing her again. His eyes had a strange intensity as he whispered hoarsely, 'Yes.'

She managed to raise an eyebrow, voice icy.

'Made it more . . . *interesting,* did it?'

His eyes never wavered, but she thought she detected pain momentarily cross them.

'Jean, believe me, I make no apology for what happened. I was overcome with desire for you but I never intended it to go as far as it did.' He faltered, then added helplessly, 'Everything moved so quickly. Afterwards I couldn't handle it, I felt so guilty — it ate into me like acid.'

He looked away, down at the table as he said slowly, deliberately, 'Now, I know only that I love you, so in one way I'm glad it happened with me but that's selfish, I know. If I had my time with you over again, it would be different, I promise. I would have held you in such respect. Controlled myself like I ought to have done.'

He looked up at her from under those eyelashes.

'All I ask is another chance.'

Jean remembered the wonder of the moment in his arms, looked again at his pleading face, at the black gleaming hair now tied back, and felt herself turning to jelly. If only . . .

But he had *not* looked at her when he had declared his love, and she could not shake the memory of what his family had done to hers. She knew that he must be cruelly playing with her.

They'd all see her go running back, clinging to him like some pathetic little creature jumping through the hoop set by the handsome Laird. Her humiliation, her family's humiliation would be complete. Then he would discard her again.

Well, it wasn't going to be like that this time . . .

Just as he had done, she lowered her eyes to her lap, couldn't face looking into his in case he saw the truth — and the deception.

'You hurt me, Adam. I don't know if I — '

His strong, hard hand, the one that had given her so much pleasure, gently covered hers as he interrupted, sensing her indecision.

'Darling, please believe me, it will be different from now on. Just the one chance to start again, that's all I ask. I've been through hell these past few hours. You won't regret it, I swear.'

Jean would have succumbed then and there — she knew. Adam Crawford was a man that any girl would have found difficult to fault; physically tall and strong, with a beautiful masculine face framed by his black hair, and those blue eyes that were even now eagerly searching hers imploringly, threatening her resolve.

She wanted this man again so badly — wanted to feel him kiss her, feel those firm lips move down over her body, feel the arousal of his manhood that would drive into her and make her his — and by so doing make *him* a part of *her*: wanted all this with a growing desire that threatened all her plans.

And then help came with his next words as,

sensing she was coming around, he continued:

'Darling, there is so little we know about each other. I want to know everything, every little detail about you — your favourite food, favourite colour; your parents, your family — especially about them. I hear your mother was a local girl — a Johnson.'

She smiled then, a sad, humourless smile because it was as she feared. He *was* using her.

'Adam, it would take us all night . . . '

He raised her hand in his and gave it a squeeze.

'Does that mean you've forgiven me?'

She lied — didn't she? Even at that moment she wasn't sure.

'Yes.'

The relief crossed his face. Beaming, he said, 'You can't begin to believe how wonderful it is to hear you say that. Let's have some supper in the restaurant — just the two of us. There's so much to talk about because . . . ' He paused, placed his other hand so hers was between his. 'Jean, there isn't much time before you go back is there — *if* you go back?'

Despite her better judgment her heart missed a beat. Adam was suggesting . . . what? She wouldn't be going because they would be together — forever?

As she nodded her consent, and watched the warmth in his eyes, she heard him say, I'll get us a table,' and saw him walk away towards the restaurant. It was all like a dream. Except deep down, she *knew* it was a nightmare.

Jean agonized over what was happening. At face value it was everything she could want in this world.

Yet a part of her knew — refused — to be taken in.

He came back, the happiness on his face transforming it into a boyishness that was even more endearing — even more difficult to cope with in its suggestion of vulnerability.

'I've got us a quiet corner.'

She followed the dining room manager past all the tables, including several of her fellow tourists who all looked appraisingly at Adam. There were some knowing looks exchanged, and Jean was convinced she saw one woman nudge her companion.

They took their seats, Jean noting that Adam had more of the view across the room towards the entrance. Was he making sure he could be seen, and could in turn watch the antics of his cronies?

The waiter came and lit the white candle. The warm glow flickered on his face, the shadows changing with every small movement of his head. With his hair as long and tied back as it was, the candlelight gave him an eighteenth-century look.

He led her through the menu, explaining the local dishes, his enthusiasm and obvious happiness puzzling her, it seemed so achingly real. The sommelier came. Adam didn't ask her anything other than whether she wanted red or white. She liked his firm decision-making for both of them.

When the sommelier returned, he showed him the label, then decanted a small amount from the bottle for him to taste. Without pretension Adam savoured the smell, and took a sip.

'Yes — thank you.'

Jean watched the rich red liquid as it rose in her glass, the candlelight reflecting red shafts off the sides.

Adam murmured, 'To us.'

Gently she allowed their glasses to touch. It was all so perfect.

6

Jean spent the next hour in a miserable, unreal state, finding herself dining intimately with the one man in the world who knew her like no other — who had seen her — *been* with her in the depths of wild abandonment . . . And yet? In truth it seemed he was not the person she had thought he was. A lump came in her throat. It was all so unfair.

On and on, all evening warning voices kept whispering in her mind as she sat opposite him enjoying his company, pretending to be warm, and friendly.

But something happened that abruptly brought her back to harsh reality.

They had just finished their dessert when he said, 'Darling, I've got to make a quick phone call — it's business. Will you excuse me for just a moment?'

Jean was taken by surprise, and then realized what it must be all about. It was an excuse to tell the others how it was going. Or perhaps it *was* a genuine call to someone — some other *woman*, explaining why he wasn't able to show up that night.

It came at just the right time, just as her

resolve was beginning to disintegrate.

'Of course.'

She looked at her watch, and said as casually as she could, 'Bit late for business, isn't it?'

Something crossed his face — she couldn't be sure what. But he was definitely uncomfortable as he mumbled, 'Oh, it's just somebody I said I'd get back to — about tomorrow. I won't be a minute.'

She watched as he got up, laid his napkin on the table, leaned over her and chuckled softly into her ear,

'Now, don't go away, will you?'

She watched his tall figure and square shoulders weave slowly between the tables and disappear from sight.

Immediately, she jumped up and made her way to the lobby, checking quickly to make sure he wasn't around. To the girl on reception who had obviously just come on duty she snapped, 'Give me my bill, please — I'm leaving at once.'

Feeling somewhat dramatic and daft she added lamely, 'There is illness in the family back home. I need a taxi immediately for Glasgow — will that be possible?'

The girl checked with a list behind the counter.

'I'll just find out.'

Jean looked nervously around, and was suddenly perturbed to see Adam coming down one of the corridors — he hadn't seen her yet.

'I'm going to the powder room — won't be a second.'

The receptionist nodded as she used the telephone.

Jean walked away quickly, turned and managed to meet Adam as if she was coming from the restaurant.

She smiled. 'Just going to the little girls' room — see you at the table.'

From the doorway she watched as he went back inside.

Jean returned to the desk. The receptionist was apologetic, the telephone still at her ear.

'I'm sorry, but for a taxi to Glasgow it will be about an hour, madam. The only one prepared to go that far at this time of night is tied up for the moment.'

Jean pressed her lips together, fought back the disappointment at not being able to get away as soon as she had had her revenge. Well, if it had to be strung out a bit, so be it. She also knew that despite everything, she would no doubt cry on and off all the way to the airport.

'That's okay. I'll be in my room when it gets here.'

The girl said yes, that would be fine, and then set down the phone and laid Jean's computerized bill on the desk before her.

'If you'd just like to check this?'

Jean shook her head and took the pen. 'That's all right. You've got my credit card impress, haven't you?'

Adam was at the table when she returned, just re-filling their glasses. As he half stood while she settled into her chair she smiled sweetly at him and said, 'Everything all right?'

'Yes — now.'

He raised his glass. 'A toast.'

She took her own, made a mental note not to drink too much more and clinked glasses with him as he declared, 'To us — and the future.'

She watched him over the rim of her glass; watched as the firm lips parted and the red liquid flowed into that part of him that she knew so well, its taste, its feel . . .

She shook herself and took a gulp of the self same wine.

He lowered his glass. 'Let's dance.'

She would have said no, and made some excuse if there had been time, but she found herself being led to the small floor even as she grappled with the thought that this was a dangerous development.

And as his large hand cupped her waist and

drew her in and slightly up to him so that her stomach touched his, something akin to an electric shock seemed to run through her body. Her legs felt weak, but there was no danger she would fall from his grasp.

She wasn't consciously aware of when her head rested against his chest and she smelt the warmth of his body, the masculine aroma of shaving soap and clean sweat that mingled with her own perfume; or heard the steady thump of his heart; or when she was finally made aware of the effect her own body was having on his.

They moved through all the slow numbers without a word.

Was it cunning design on her part, a final act of revenge or the unstoppable urge of her own femininity that made her finally murmur, 'Let's go to my room?'

He paused, and asked nervously, 'Are you sure?'

She nodded and they moved back to the table.

Jean felt tense with excitement, still unsure of her motive.

Either way, whether it was an urge to crown her victory over him or a genuine reaction to how she felt at that moment, she could at least enjoy his magnificent body one last time. She picked up her handbag from beside her chair and led the way to the stairs. Alongside, Adam leisurely took the steps two at a time. At the top he drew nearer, put his arm around her and let his hand rest on her opposite hip in a loose, but clear statement of ownership. At any other time it would have felt good.

At her bedroom door he smiled down at her, held her chin gently between his finger and thumb.

'Jean, I love you. We don't need to do this.'

She pouted up at him with, 'Don't you want to make love to me?'

'Of course, but — '

Once again she cut him off, putting her own finger on those adorable lips.

'Shhh.'

She seemed unable to get the key into the lock so he took it from her and opened the door himself. It was only then that, with a shock, Jean realized what she was truly proposing to do.

He led the way, moving into the room as she closed the door and leant back against it, dropping her bag to the floor. Slowly, with measured movements she stripped naked, taking in with satisfaction the at first stunned, then appreciative and then finally, as she pushed away her silk panties and they fell to her ankles, frankly unbridled admiration and lust in those deep blue eyes. He started to remove his jacket but Jean's blood now roared in her ears as she knew what she wanted — what she had to do.

Even then, though, some tiny part of her mind reflected momentarily on the change that had come over her as she stepped up to him as naked as the day she was born, now without any sense of shyness, happy and confident in her own body, proud of the effect it was having on him; would on any man. She was already a different woman to the one that had arrived such a short time ago.

She smiled but her voice was firm and almost harsh, as she ordered, 'No.'

She took hold of his coat, pulled it roughly down to his elbows, effectively pinning them to his sides, though his hands rested on her hips.

Jean removed his tie and threw it aside, taking her time as she unbuttoned his shirt, running her hands through the hair of his chest, before she pulled the shirt down over his wide shoulders to join the jacket. His clear blue eyes never left hers. She stared back at him, knowing that they could read in them what she was going to do next.

She leaned in again, kissed his chest, ran her tongue over his skin as she sank to her knees, tasting the little beads of perspiration.

Slowly she undid his trousers, unbuckling the belt and pulling down the zipper with slow deliberation, before hooking her thumbs into both trousers and briefs and dragging them down around his knees.

She faced his manhood, felt its heat against her cheek.

For a few fleeting seconds she closed her eyes, heard him groaning as she instinctively did what she felt was natural.

Abruptly, knowing she had to stop, she stood up. With his cords and briefs still around his legs she pushed him back onto the bed and crouched on top of him, curled feet under his firm buttocks.

As Jean sank onto his upthrusting hips she pulled his hair free so that the mane of black straddled the sheet beside his face, then pinned his arms to the bed with her own.

She leaned nearer, so her hanging breasts just touched his chest; watched his face, pleased with what she saw there as she let her hardened nipples glide gently from side to side across his flat, muscular chest, enjoying every delicious second of the torture she was inflicting upon him.

Suddenly she drew nearer, crushed her breasts hard against him.

For several minutes Jean did what she

liked, exploring the helpless, magnificent body, biting the side of his neck, kissing his leathery cheek, feeling the fine stubble just beneath the soap-tasting skin; teasingly brushing the sides of his mouth with her lips, then covering it with her own, forcing her way in and exploring his teeth, the insides of his cheeks; finding his tongue, which was in turn pushed back into her as she suffered the same searching probe of her mouth until she pulled away, all the time thrusting and lifting her own body with an ever-faster pounding of flesh on flesh until she had to bite back a scream as she reached the highest point of animal pleasure.

But the torture was not over — at least, not for her.

Effortlessly, in a move that served to show that he had been a prisoner only of the passion inspired by her advances, rather than her physical strength, he sat up, took her weight around the waist and moved to the edge of the bed as they were still locked together. There, his strong arms wrapped around her in an embrace that would have been impossible to break — not that she tried — and he once more made her body ride again, head back, hair flowing wildly, eyes closed, gasping as his lips and teeth pulled and kissed and teased in time to the increasing motion of love.

The pleasure and pain made her scream out — scream to stop, scream to go on forever.

Then, with one final shuddering thrust he held her so tightly to him that it should have been painful, yet now was not hard enough. She wanted to be squeezed so tight that she would pass into him, *be* him.

He clung to her for several seconds, holding his breath, before releasing it with an explosion of air, and collapsing backwards.

They came gently to rest, side by side.

Afterwards, this time, there was no pain, no anger, no recriminations from him. For both of them there was only an overriding sense that the act of love had been more than mere passion, more than just the sexual act.

There had been something else.

Neither spoke for a long while; only their ragged breathing filled the otherwise silent room.

Wonderingly, Jean noted that their hair — his black, hers auburn — mingled on the white pillow beside their heads, entwined and joined as their bodies had been seconds before.

Her eyes became moist, and a lump came to her throat at what could have been — what *should* have been.

Minutes passed. She wasn't even sure if she had dozed or not before he whispered in her ear, 'Darling, are you all right?'

His concerned voice brought her back to reality. She blinked back the moisture.

'That was beautiful.'

He nodded, stroked a fine strand from the corner of her mouth, tracing his finger delicately up her face, back to her mass of hair.

'It was as it should be, as it always will be — now.'

Jean fought back the tears, felt her resolve of the last few hours beginning to evaporate completely.

She looked away, couldn't face him as he continued: 'With you, Jean, it's so different. I feel . . . ' He paused, obviously finding it difficult to select the right words. It was apparent that to express himself in this way was normally alien to him.

'It's hard to explain, but . . . ' he looked sheepishly at her, ' . . . promise you won't laugh?'

'Of course not,' she admonished him.

'It's . . . it's as if I've found the other half of my own body.' He grimaced. 'No, that's not what I mean. It's like I've found the part of me that's always been missing — a sort of completeness.' He stared at her.

'It's as if I've been waiting all my life for this, even beyond my own self, my own existence. I feel a great sense of relief that something is all over, that I'm reunited with my past. And it's all because of you.'

Jean lay there, utterly devastated. Adam Crawford was murmuring sentiments to her that could only mean one of two things:

That he truly was in *love* with her — for what else was he talking about when he spoke of finding his other self, something spiritual, the communion of souls as well as flesh, that they were soulmates?

Or something else?

Was he playing with her, trying to get her to say things that he could laugh about later, the final humiliation of her, and her family?

He leaned forward, kissed her so lightly so delicately on the cheek that for a moment she didn't realize what had happened.

It was then that Jean *realized* that he was in love with her . . . just as he said.

'Perhaps your parents can see us now?'

She sat up, and pulled away.

'Why did you say that?'

He raised his head and held it with his hand, his elbow on the bed.

'Well — you know — they would see you were happy. That's all I meant.'

'But they're dead!'

'I know. Kath told me.' Puzzled, he reached out to her and touched her cheek with the back of his curled fingers.

'What's the matter, darling? I meant it in a nice way.'

Jean pushed his hand away, and jumped out of bed, pulling the sheet around her.

'Why did you bring the family back into this?'

It was his turn to frown with exasperation.

'I don't understand. All I meant was, we are so happy it would have been nice if they could see it as well. And hopefully, if there is any meaning to this life, there is something else to look forward to — and they're watching over us right now.'

Jean stood at the window holding the sheet tightly to her bosom, looking out into the night. She could just see a few small lights on what would be the far shore of the loch. It seemed appropriate, like the far shore of that journey they would all make one day. Perhaps one of the lights was Braemore?

Abruptly she said, 'What's the mystery of Braemore House, Adam? You know the place I mean.'

For the first time he took his eyes off her, seemed to be avoiding hers as she looked directly at him, one eyebrow raised in expectation.

He drawled uncomfortably, 'Mystery? What do you mean?'

She snapped, 'Who does it belong to? Who lives there — if anybody?'

He didn't immediately say anything, so she added accusingly, 'What's its history?'

He sat up, swung his muscled legs to the floor and padded slowly towards the bathroom, seeming to imply in his easy nakedness that he had nothing to hide from her even if *she* had to wrap herself in the sheet — enclosing her own inhibitions and secrets.

'It's a long story — but I don't understand why you're bringing it up now, and becoming so agitated. We were having such a lovely time.'

Something burnt fiercely inside her at the memory of the way last time she had been having a lovely time and he had thrust a knife through her heart.

An innate cunning took hold. She brightened, let the sheet slip to the floor, walked into his path and blocked the doorway. Without her heels he towered even larger over her. She went up onto her toes, reached up her arms and wrapped them around the back of his neck, tangling her hands into his hair, at the same time pressing her naked body against his.

Despite everything it was still the most

magnificent of feelings.

'I'm sorry, darling. Why don't you have a lovely hot bath — I'll scrub your back.'

Relief and happiness came back to his eyes. He looked tenderly down at her, teased, 'Maybe I will — if you'll join me?'

She grinned, playfully jerked his hair. 'I thought you'd never ask. Of course I will — but you go first. I'll order drinks while I pin up my hair. What would you like?'

'I'll have a Bacardi and Coke.'

He went in, half closing the door. She listened as the taps began to roar, fiddled with her hair for a second until she was sure he was sitting in the bath, could hear him splashing around and then begin to sing.

Jean scrambled into her clothes and was reaching for the phone when it rang, making her jump. It was reception — her taxi had arrived.

After the initial shock she turned it to her advantage, saying loudly, 'Of course, I'll be right down.'

She put her head around the door, careful not to let him see her clothes.

'I'm just popping down to reception — they need me to help with an old lady from back home. Have a good soak, I won't be a second.'

She blew a kiss, quickly closing the door

before he could say anything.

In seconds she had her luggage in the corridor, then went back and looked around.

She couldn't quantify her emotions, which now exploded out of her like a burst dam. She cried, partly with loss, at what she was doing — leaving the man who meant so much to her in so many different ways; crying at the hurt she was causing herself.

Or was it at her loss because Adam was deceiving her, all this talk of her family revealing his real intention: further humiliation?

The latter finally gained the upper hand. Sobbing with anger she kicked at his trousers, then suddenly on impulse gathered all his clothes, opened the window and flung them out into the night.

She was still crying as the taxi swung out of the hotel drive. Jean looked over her shoulder at the retreating lights.

It was the end of the most beautiful and yet the most traumatic time in her life.

7

There was a four-hour delay at Glasgow airport before she could catch a flight to New York where she would have to change planes.

It was as she was sitting huddled miserably over a cup of coffee that she suddenly remembered Kath, her friend of so little time yet the one person in the world she felt she could — and should — confide in.

Although it was the middle of the night, she felt guilty at having left so abruptly, without saying goodbye, but there really hadn't been the time, and in any case, she had been somewhat emotionally shell-shocked.

Jean fed the money into the phone and dialled the number she had been given. It was answered in seconds, the soft accent instantly recognizable as that of her friend.

'Oh Kath, it's me.' She didn't have to say anything more.

'Jean, where are you? I've been so worried about you.'

'Glasgow — on . . . on my way back home.'

'My God, what's happened?'

With difficulty, occasionally with a sob that couldn't be smothered, Jean told her everything, her throat constricted and sore for being tensed up for so long.

'So there you are, it's not to be. Kath — have I done the right thing?'

Her friend's voice showed her concern.

'Jean, what can I say? After you left, all hell broke loose.'

Jean felt her chest tighten with fear.

'Why — what happened?'

There was a pause and then Kath continued.

'Well, apparently Adam came rushing down into reception with only a towel wrapped around his waist. There was a terrible scene. He kept shouting for you. When they told him you'd left he went wild, and ran out of the hotel.'

Jean knew she should have felt triumphant; she had avenged the way she had been treated, the way her family had been badly used by the Crawfords.

But it was a hollow victory. In the process she had lost something that might have been the most precious thing in the world — true love.

Had he any feelings for her? He couldn't have faked it all, surely?

But now she would never know.

Her throat ached so badly she couldn't speak.

It was Kath who eventually said,

'You still there, Jean?'

'Yes,' she managed hoarsely, and finally added, 'I've got to go. I'll keep in touch, Kath — I enjoyed our short friendship very much. Perhaps you could come and visit me in the States?

'Me too. I'd like that very much. Maybe we'll see you back in Scotland sometime?'

Jean shook her head at the wall before her.

'No, Kath, I don't think I will ever come back. There's been too much pain already.'

Kath sounded tearful. 'I understand. Well, let me know when you get back safely won't you?'

'Yes of course. And Kath . . . ' Jean was only just struck by the idea, 'Kath, will you be my bridesmaid?'

The tears finally broke through as the reply came. 'Oh Jean — really?'

'Yes! And don't worry about the fare and everything — we'll make it part of the wedding expenses. What's a few dollars more for Don anyway; he and his father are rolling in it.'

'But there must be girls at home you should be asking first . . . ?'

Jean said firmly, mind completely made up.

'Kath — I want *you*. I'll write, okay?'

'Oh thank you, Jean — and it will be wonderful to see you again.'

'And you, Kath. Goodbye.' She swallowed. 'Give my love to everybody in Inverdee.'

They were both in tears when she rang off.

Finally as dawn came with an ugly yellow smear in a cloudy sky the flight was called.

Jean boarded the plane and buckled herself into the window seat.

Eventually the engines were switched on, the faint far-off whine accompanied the vibration that ran through her seat, and into the pit of her stomach. Whilst she didn't have a phobia about flying, it was also definitely not her favourite occupation. But this time her mind soon went elsewhere. Even when the doors were closed and with a mild jolt the plane was manoeuvred backwards, she really wasn't tense. There was only the desire to get on with it.

Released from the grip of the marshalling wagon the plane's engines roared as it swung around and taxied past the terminal.

It was only then that Jean saw the figure running along the observation roof of the airport building; the unmistakeably tall figure with black hair blowing wildly in the rain-swept wind.

'Oh my God!' She said it aloud.

They gathered speed as they cleared the other parked aircraft, leaving the figure dwindling into the morning gloom, arms gesticulating wildly.

Was he angry — or beseeching? She couldn't make up her mind.

Finally he was lost from sight, and as they sped down the runway and lifted off, free of the shackles of earth, he was no more.

8

By the time she had flown down to Fort Worth, Dallas and waited around for a very surprised Don, Jean was drained of all emotion. Fatigued and jet-lagged she met him even as he parked his Cadillac and got out.

He was quite tall, his shock of blond hair cut short, hidden by a wide-brimmed cowboy hat that looked somewhat incongruous with his formal business suit.

He gave her a quick kiss on the cheek then reached out and took her luggage.

As he carried it around to the trunk he said, 'What in the hell are you doing back so quick?'

It was not what she expected, but perhaps he could be forgiven — after all, it must have been a shock to get her call from New York. Still, since he hadn't wanted her to go in the first place, surely her quick return should have delighted him?

On the phone she had just said that the hotel was awful, food awful, weather awful.

She tried a white lie.

'I missed you.'

Courteously he held the door for her to get in.

'Well, I sure as hell missed you, honey.'

Guilt began to well up dangerously inside her. For all his lack of excitement, in some ways, Don was a decent man, didn't deserve to be treated the way he had. Jean resolved to bury the time in Scotland, her Highland Interlude, in the back of her mind, pretend even that it had never happened. But that, she realized, would be impossible. Whatever else had transpired, and for whatever reason, Adam Crawford was the first man she had carnal knowledge of — and that was a milestone that no woman could ever entirely obliterate from her mind.

Feeling suddenly sorry for herself she said, 'Don, let's not wait any longer, let's get married right away.'

He looked at her as he reversed out of the parking lot.

'Hell, you've changed, Jean.'

He stopped the car.

'You don't even look the same. What have you been up to?'

She went as red as the car's bodywork and gasped with shock.

'For God's sake, Don, I thought you'd be pleased.'

He put the automatic into drive and stood

on the gas. With a squeal of tyres they lurched forward.

He gesticulated with his free hand. 'Hell, I've got everything arranged. You know I can't take time off just like that.'

Jean shrank down in the seat, feeling the cold hands of normality dragging her back into the real world.

'Surely your father can arrange something?'

It was unfair, she realized that even before she said it, but it made no difference.

Don shot her a hard glance. 'You're in a sure-fire hurry all of a sudden! If it's that bad, why don't we just start setting up house together right away?'

Jean knew what he meant — that she should move in with him at his place — like he had always wanted and she had doggedly refused to do up to now.

'You know I can't do that, Don.'

For her age and the times they lived in she was strangely innocent. She grunted inwardly — *had* been innocent. Maybe it was because her father had been in the Services and they had moved around a bit, so that as an only child she had read a lot — a diet of high romance and tempestuous love affairs: *Pride and Prejudice, Jane Eyre* and *Wuthering Heights* were her all-time favourites.

So, consciously or unconsciously, she had

saved herself for the 'right' man and marriage.

And then look what had happened. Like one of her heroines she had succumbed in the most precipitous way, screaming into the night sky as she changed from a girl to a woman with a man she really didn't know.

As Don droned on about work and other things, she closed her eyes. It was all too much. She had to sleep.

But it wouldn't come. She turned to her side, away from him, pretending, because she didn't want to talk.

Instead, for mile after mile she looked across the curve of the earth, at the dusty pastures of the Texas plains — so different from the heather-covered Scottish mountains sweeping down to placid lochs, or mountainous seas.

She wondered how things were in Inverdee, surreptitiously looking at her watch. Back there, it was nine o'clock in the morning of the day after she had left. The boat would just be leaving the hotel jetty now. In half an hour the first customers would be sitting down with their coffee in the little café.

It was no good — she knew where her thoughts were leading her. Would Adam be behind the counter, or would he even now be spurring his horse on with those long legs encased in tight riding breeches, urging his steed up the hillside?

Would he be working off his rage at having been outwitted by a Johnson — or nursing a broken heart?

Wishful thinking. A bit of American candour made her grimace at the thought. He was a jerk.

An hour passed when Don suddenly said, 'You awake?'

She pretended to be just stirring and pulled herself upright.

'Yes.'

'Fine company you've been.' He sounded grumpy. 'I'll drop you off home but I've got to go straight back to work. I'll see you tonight about seven — okay?'

She couldn't say no, that she'd like to be alone; it would have been churlish and ungrateful.

'Make it eight, Don please, I'll need to freshen up and have some more shut-eye.'

They pulled up at the single-storey, ranch-style building that had been home to her for the last few years.

Don busied himself as she walked alone up the path and unlocked the front door.

It was all as she had left it. There was no cheery call from the kitchen, no mother wiping her hands on her apron, appearing in the doorway; no father, braces over his shirt, pipe in mouth, newspaper in the other, greeting her from the den.

Don's white hat caught the sun as he loomed in the doorway.

'I'll take them to your room.' He moved down the corridor, filling it with his bulky frame, and went into her bedroom.

She followed, wasn't expecting it as he turned and suddenly took her by the shoulders and pressed his face down over hers. Don liked to smoke — that, she conceded, she'd have to put up with — but he also chewed a little baccy, and his mouth tasted of it now. She stood there, passively enduring as his tongue explored her mouth, not wanting to upset him but she was desperately over-tired.

Finally he pulled back, gave his special knowing wink.

Resigned to what she knew she had to do she stood perfectly still, hoping what she called his 'manly fumbling' would be quickly over.

Don had told her that was how he liked it — no participation by her — and up to now she had thought that was probably the norm.

But that was before Adam.

Now she knew otherwise.

He undid her blouse, drew it slowly aside

and back off her shoulders.

He ran his fingers down the side of her breasts, just above the edge of her bra, then dipped them under her straps and, even more slowly, drew them off.

She leant against him, her tiredness making her feel more irritated at the coldness of it all.

'Don — please, not now.'

His fingers curled under her nipples as he eased them out.

'Aw, come on, honey. Aren't they glad to see me?'

'Yes, of course, but Don, please, I'm very tired.'

Suddenly he tweaked them harshly.

Wincing, she put the flat of her hand against his chest and pushed him roughly off. His face darkened.

'Hell, I don't deserve that. What was all that shit about wanting to get married right away?'

She began to cry, trying to cover herself up at the same time.

'I'm sorry, Don, I'll be rested by tonight. Then we can talk.'

He glowered at her as he paused in the doorway.

'That's all you ever want to do — *talk*. It's about time there was a little more *action* around here.'

He stalked up the corridor as she hurried after him, pulling her clothes back around her shoulders.

'Don, I'm sorry. I'll see you tonight then . . . Don?'

The front door slammed behind him.

Depressed, Jean wandered back into her room, fell face down on the bed. A great sob wracked her body, then another. Everything seemed to well up inside.

She cried for her lost self.

She cried for her lost mother and father.

She cried for her lost love in the never-never land of her mind.

9

Jean awoke around seven with an ache in her left eye and temple, and recognized it for what it was: the beginning of a migraine.

She dragged herself to the bathroom, found the tablets her doctor had prescribed and filled a plastic mug with water.

As she tossed them back she saw her reflection in the mirror for the first time. Her skin was distorted by the imprint of the quilt on her moist cheeks. That, and the bags under her eyes and lack of make-up made her look dreadful.

Jean knew that she had been unfair to Don, and seeing herself now, realized that it was down to her to make a special effort. She leant against the basin.

Really, there was no excuse now for not letting Don have his way with her. After all, her virginity was gone, so what excuse had she in her own mind? No — there was no honest reason left.

Tonight. She would let him make love to her, and go all the way. Anything less, and she would be a hypocrite. In a funny sort of way the decision seemed to take a great weight off her mind. Some of her old resolution came back into her movements as she drew water for a hot bath, threw off her crumpled clothes and organized her make-up bag and toilet bits.

Dressed only in a light dressing gown she went to the kitchen to get a glass of milk and some cookies. Coming back through the lounge her eyes just happened to fall on the family photographs arranged on the bureau.

Something stirred inside her, made her walk over and set the glass down. There was one photograph in particular that caught her eye, a black and white one amongst all the colour. It was of her mother, at about the same age as Jean was now.

She looked intently at it for several seconds, studied every detail of the youthful face that looked back at her out of the past.

After a while her other hand found the one of herself at a similar age, taken just before they had died.

She compared the two. For the first time she could see the similarities that others had spoken about, but that she had never been able to see — or had never really *bothered* to see — hair that despite the lack of colour she knew was the same rich auburn; the nose, the ears, and above all, the eyes.

But whereas the photograph of herself

showed a rather modern version, a fully developed young woman in checked shirt and jeans, (she grunted, knowing the reality of the situation — who said the camera never lies?) the one of her mother had the appearance of an innocent young girl in a dress.

Yet it had been taken only weeks before she had met her father and begun a journey of love that had never ended — a journey that was, she was sure, going on even now, beyond the interlude that was this life.

The background, too, was different, as if to emphasize even further the difference in their situation.

Jean's photograph showed a dusty corner of the back yard, while her mother's showed that she was standing in a country lane, with the outline of hills beyond. Scotland and Texas — as different as chalk and cheese.

She kissed her mother, held it against her heart as she set her own photograph down, then tucked the other one under her arm, picked up her milk and plate and returned to the bedroom.

It took a further three quarters of an hour for the tablets and the soak in hot water to make her feel better.

Dried, she took time with her hair and face, and then finally, with half an hour to go before Don came — *if* he came after the

159

morning's debacle — she contemplated what to wear.

Sitting on the edge of her bed it was only then that she turned her mind to her fiancé and what she had decided to do.

There was a strange lack of excitement in the mechanical way she set about her task of making herself fetching for him: opening a drawer that held items of her trousseau; laying the expensive pure silk French-style panties and frothy slip on the bed before removing from their packet the silk stockings that went with the lacy belt and brassiere. There seemed no point in holding them back for her wedding night now.

After dressing she stepped into her high-heeled court shoes, and ruefully contemplated the finished 'article' in her full-length mirror. My God, she thought. Talk about a dog's dinner! She allowed one knee to cross in front of the other, hands on hips as she struck the classic pouting vamp's pose.

While everything was right, and she looked, she thought, as good as she ever would in that department, something was lacking.

It still was, even when she drew on her see-through peignoir that underlined the feminine delights awaiting any man — or to be precise, Don — who set his eyes on her dressed like this.

And then it dawned on her what was wrong — what was *missing:* it was all so lacking in emotion.

There was no inner fire; she radiated no sultriness, no passion in her sexuality.

She was a woman posing in sexy clothes, *not* a lover dressing for her man.

The realization made her sit down heavily on her dressing table stool and stare blankly at her face in the mirror.

She felt like crying — but after the events of the last few days, there were no more tears left.

Still, the full understanding of what she was finally contemplating slowly set in.

Don was not the man for her — never would be! It was better to do the right thing now, before it was too late, than regret it for the rest of her — and *his* — lifetime.

Maybe if she hadn't gone to Scotland, met Adam Crawford, and for whatever the reason, tasted what, for her at least, had been true passion, maybe things would have been different. What was that old saying her mother used to come out with from time to time — 'What you don't know about, you'll never miss'? Something like that. Maybe they would have had a good life as man and wife, certainly as good as some couples she knew, especially if and when the kids came along.

Not all couples knew such ecstasy. In the normal, everyday world they just got by as best as they were able. Love could grow over the years just by shared joy, shared sorrow, and shared time.

Could.

But for her she knew it would not work. She had tasted the forbidden fruit — a truly passionate experience with a man that her desire for had, at the time, consumed her wholly, so that later the betrayal had nearly destroyed her.

Jean knew that the memory of Adam would blight for always her life together with Don. Maybe she wouldn't *want* to compare Don's lovemaking, but as sure as there was a heaven above, it would always be at the back of her mind, eating away like a cancer at their relationship. Her mind made up, she decided she would change into jeans and a T-shirt, tell him everything, straight away.

She was shaken out of her thoughts by the door chime. She jumped up and looked at her watch. Good Lord, it was eight o'clock, and he was right on time. She flew down the corridor, and swung the door open.

'Don, come in.'

He was holding some flowers in one hand, a bottle of wine in the other; the white Dallas cowboy hat was still on his head, making him look for all the world like J.R. Ewing.

He seemed stunned, his gaze taking her in from head to toe before he spoke with a whistle.

'Baby, you look terrific!'

He stepped inside the hallway and closed the door with his foot as she stumbled backwards, acutely aware of the wrong impression she must be giving.

'Thank you, Don. I — '

He held out the flowers. 'These are for you, gal, and this . . . is for both of us.'

It was only then that she saw that it was real French champagne.

Jean took the flowers as he continued to lovingly appraise her. Protectively, she pulled the peignoir closer around her body as he whistled again.

'Wowee, you're some classy dame when you put your mind to it.'

Jean smiled weakly. 'I'll put these in water.'

She was conscious of his eyes on her back as she went into the kitchen, found a vase and filled it with water, all the time grappling with the problem of how to tell him that it would not work out — that she had changed, and was no longer the girl he had proposed to. He would make somebody a wonderful husband, it just wouldn't be her.

She almost jumped out of her shoes as the

cork shot out of the bottle and hit the ceiling behind her.

Don let out a cowboy's 'Yee-ha!' of delight and poured the bubbling liquid into two glasses, handing one to her.

'There you go. Get that down your pretty little throat.'

She couldn't help but take the offered glass, struggled with the idea of telling him then and there. She knew it had to be soon but panicked, took a gulp to help her.

He drank his glass down in one go and re-filled it to the brim.

'Come on, little one, get that down you. We've got some celebrating to do. My God, I thought I was gonna have to work real hard tonight . . . '

He used a finger of one hand holding the bottle to propel the bottom of her glass up so that she had to take another large drink to stop it spilling.

Jean knew that it had already gone far enough, and the only thing she could do was to quickly get out of those ridiculous clothes, and come back to confront him in jeans and a top or something.

'Don — stay there, I won't be a minute.'

In the bedroom she stopped for another quick gulp for Dutch courage, set the glass down and pulled off the peignoir . . .

When his large hands grasped her shoulders from behind and his mouth came down to the root of her neck, she actually gave a small scream of fright.

'Don — stop it!'

He ignored her pleas, slid his arms around her waist, his hands on her belly pulling her back against him. She could feel his hardness through the thin silk of the slip.

'No!'

Jean struggled to release herself, managed to half turn. His hands seemed to be everywhere, not making love, just roughly probing, pinching, and tickling.

With a rush of fear she could smell beer; he had been drinking before he came round to her.

It registered, just as he suddenly realized she really wasn't going to let him continue, that she wasn't just playing hard to get. He held her by the wrists.

'Stop teasing me, you bitch!'

The more she struggled, the harsher he became until he suddenly stepped back, pinned both her arms together with one of his, raised his other hand and with a back swing slapped the side of her face, sending her flying onto the bed on her front.

Before she had time to recover from the shock, he grasped the back of her neck with one hand, held her struggling, face tightly pressed into the pillow.

She could hardly breathe.

Jean knew real terror then as with the other, he ripped her slip up. Her body jerked as he plucked off the French panties, dispensing with them in one snatch that shredded them in two.

She, like all American girls, knew what date rape was, knew that in court they would ask her why she was expecting him, dressed like she was, and drinking his champagne to boot to celebrate their forthcoming marriage, if it wasn't because she expected intimacy to occur.

But she *knew* she was screaming: 'No. No. No.'

Over and over again.

10

Just as she finally gave up hope, thought it was too late, the doorbell chimed and a voice called out from inside the hall: 'Jean, are you there? I've let myself in — somebody said you were back so I've called to see if you need anything. I couldn't believe it — are you all right?'

It was her neighbour from down the road, a dear old lady she had befriended when her husband had been admitted to hospital.

Footsteps sounded right outside the bedroom door.

Don jumped up and ran into the en-suite bathroom as Jean rolled off the bed and struggled to wrap a dressing gown around her shaking body.

She met Mrs O'Neil in the corridor.

'Jean — oh there you are, my dear. Are you all right? You're home so soon.'

Jean went to the dumpy, white-haired woman, threw her arms around her and held on tight.

Momentarily, Mrs O'Neil looked shocked, but then instinctively stroked her hair, cooing gently as she mothered her like a child.

'There there, my dear, whatever is the matter?'

Jean finally managed to pull herself together and stand back.

'Everything's all right now, I promise. Will you stay — have a cup of coffee? I've got so much to tell you.'

The little old lady beamed. 'Of course, my dear, I'd love to.'

Jean nodded at the kitchen. 'Would you mind getting the pot going while I get some clothes on? I won't be a second.'

She closed the kitchen door and hurried back to her bedroom.

Don stood in the room glowering.

'Stupid old crone. If it wasn't for her we would be having a real good time. Can't you get rid of her quick?'

Jean could hardly believe what she was hearing! What had been for her a terrible experience, was, it seemed, considered by Don to be . . . love making.

The truth dawned on her that they were poles apart, that for all his urbane civilized exterior, Don was a crude, uncouth, uncaring man who only saw women as something to be used. She knew that however awful the experience, it had been God-sent — revealing the man in his true colours but delivering her in time from the final degradation.

When it came, her own voice was alien even to her, a low, bitter hiss that she had never heard before, its effect on him like the physical slap in the face that he had given her.

'Get out of this house and never, ever come back! If I ever even so much as hear from you again I'll . . . '

Her voice tailed off, but the menace born of a madness was such that even he could detect it; see it in her eyes.

He picked up his hat, said nothing until he reached the front door, which Mrs O'Neil had left open.

He paused, and half turned.

'You'll be sorry about this. You can't just stand me up and make me look a fool, believe me.'

Jean pushed the door against him but he didn't budge, just remained rock still, staring down at her.

Jean's chin came up in defiance.

'Move, or I'll call the police.'

His lip curled up in a sardonic grin. 'What are you gonna say — decked out like some whore waiting for me. You didn't know what you were doing?'

The stand-off lasted another ten seconds that seemed like a lifetime before he put on his hat.

'I'll see you, Jean . . . that's a promise.'

There was menace in the soft drawl. He grinned again.

'Pity. You were looking real good.'

He took a leisurely step out and the door slammed shut, leaving Jean leaning back against it, shaking like a leaf, chest heaving from shock and exertion.

Only when she heard his car drive away did she manage to collect herself and return to the kitchen.

To the expectant Mrs O'Neil she said that Don had just left, upset that their engagement was off. But she said nothing of the awful manner of its ending.

Quickly she changed the subject, telling Mrs O'Neil, whose parents had come from Ireland, how beautiful Scotland was, about her brief stay there and how friendly the people were, and especially about her new friend, Kath.

But Mrs O'Neil looked puzzled.

'It all sounds marvellous — so why are you home so swiftly? There's something more, isn't there, my dear?'

Silently Jean nodded. The old lady took her hand and patted it.

'Spill it out, my dear, you'll feel better.'

Jean told her then of her tempestuous first act of love — surprised at her own frankness

— and about, for her at least, its sad and abrupt end.

The old lady listened intently, and for some time afterwards remained quiet and still, obviously thinking. Then she said, 'It seems to me, my dear, that you have been a very lucky girl. My advice is to forget your pride; there seems to have been something special between you despite everything — real or imaginary. This family thing seems to have loomed overly large in your mind. Why don't you write to him, set out what you feel? You never know, you might get a nice surprise.'

Those words went over and over in her mind as she showered, letting the running water cleanse her body of all memory of its contact with Don's.

Could she really write to Adam after what she had done? Although she ached inside at the thought of him, her pride would be an insurmountable obstacle.

When she stepped out of the cubicle and dried off, she gave herself a cursory inspection. Apart from a red welt on her cheek that would probably be gone by the next day and some bruises that would be out of sight under her clothes, nobody would guess what had happened. She pulled on jeans and a T-shirt.

The remains of her trousseau she took

outside and threw in the garbage can, then she sat on her old swing in the corner of the yard, gently rocking herself with one foot on the ground as she contemplated the dusk, and the twinkling lights of the town.

If what had occurred with Don had happened, say, a week earlier, it would have been even more disastrous. With no other experience as a yardstick to measure against, she would have assumed that his behaviour was the norm.

She shuddered at the thought.

With that sort of a man, instinct told her, things would not improve. Quite the reverse.

Her mind returned again to Adam and Mrs O'Neil's advice, and the knowledge that she could never just send a letter to him — not after what she had done!

Her heart leapt. There was a way round it! She would be writing to Kath, telling her the wedding was off, so she could let her know more about how she regretted the way it had ended with Adam. Kath might be able to pass on the fact, see if there was any hope . . .

It was asking a lot of a friend but Jean knew Kath would do it for her.

She spent the rest of the evening curled up on the sofa, discarded plate of half-eaten chilli on one side, a TV game show — with the volume turned down — on in the corner, writing and re-writing until finally, at one in the morning, she was satisfied.

She re-read it for the umpteenth time, carefully checking the casualness of how she got round to the subject of Adam. Then came the sixty-four thousand dollar question: would Kath be able to accidentally bump into him, say, at the tea shop, and bring her name up in conversation? Jean felt slightly sick in the pit of her stomach. Suppose he was really contemptuous of her after what she had done; that there was no hope at all?

She fell into a troubled sleep and awoke with a stiff neck at 4 a.m. It was only as she routinely locked the front door and checked the windows that she remembered Don.

And his threat to see her again.

11

The morning was bright, the hard Texas sun up early as she drove to the hospital and checked in with the nursing supervisor. Short-staffed due to an outbreak of a flu-like virus, they welcomed her back early with open arms.

As a scrub nurse in the O.R. she was soon assisting the surgeons with a complicated procedure that would, if it worked, repair an elderly man's hand function.

Consequently, she had little time for herself and the letter didn't get posted that day, or the next. It was only on the third day that she acknowledged to herself that it wasn't *just* because she was busy, that she was using that as an excuse. She was afraid to send it because she was afraid of the answer Kath would give her.

Whilst things were left as they were, she had had a short, wonderful, but finally sad love affair, which she had left of her own volition. It had been *her* decision. The memory, and more importantly, the hope of renewal, would still be there for weeks, months, years — always.

But the moment she posted the letter she knew that she would be losing control, placing her fate into Adam Crawford's hands, courting rejection that would ruin the memory forever.

And she wanted that memory.

It was all she had now.

A few days later she took the crumpled letter from her purse and opened it. No, she hadn't expressed herself properly. She re-wrote it, carried it around with her for several more days, during which time she was asked if she would switch to night duty for the next week.

It suited Jean; she wasn't sleeping well at all.

On the first night alone, at the nurses' station, dressed in her white uniform and small cap, her feet in white shoes tucked under the stool she was sitting on, she slipped out the envelope from her side pocket and examined it in the pool of light from the desk lamp.

Wearily, she turned it over and wondered about changing it yet again, wondered even about writing to Adam directly. She took the stethoscope draped over her neck and shoulders and placed it carefully to one side.

In the depths of the night it seemed a good

time to write down feelings that at other times she might not be able to articulate. She pulled out a sheet of hospital paper and took a pen from her hip pocket. She'd write them down now, wouldn't necessarily be sending them to him — at least not yet — but they would be there, waiting.

Jean had never realized before that she was capable of such a thing, as sometime later as the sun crept into the eastern sky, she re-read what she had penned.

She actually blushed.

It dawned on her then that it gave her a remarkable insight into the change she had gone through — sudden, quantifiable, proof of how far she had moved emotionally in the last few weeks.

She was relieved of duty at eight o'clock. The morning was already humid and she started to perspire as she walked across the parking lot to her car.

It was as she was getting in, slinging her bag across to the passenger seat, that she saw him. Don was sitting in his car, looking directly at her. As soon as he saw that she had noticed him he started up the engine and drove away, passing in front of her but looking straight ahead.

Jean sat in the car, trying to calm herself down. He had every right to be there; perhaps he'd just dropped somebody off — his old daddy, perhaps, who wasn't in the best of health.

All the same, as she started the car and switched on the air conditioning, she noticed her perspiration had become a full-on sweat.

The letter to Kath, though not her lines to Adam, she posted on the way home.

*   *   *

The week began, and at the start of her first day shift she checked her mailbox, searching eagerly through the letters for one with a British stamp. As the week progressed, excited anticipation turned to disappointment, disappointment to depression and finally to desperation.

She contemplated calling Inverdee on the phone, and then kept deciding against it. If nobody could be bothered with her, why the hell should she embarrass and humiliate herself even more?

Jean snorted, tossing back the mane of auburn hair that was now growing a little unkempt. She knew, too, even without Mrs O'Neil's worried motherly concern, that she was losing weight. Her cheekbones seemed a little more prominent, her eyes a little more fierce when she was angry — which seemed to be happening more often, especially when she was exasperated with student nurses who didn't follow her instructions to the letter. Behind her back she was talked about as suddenly having a short fuse.

None of it was like her.

Eventually, Jean no longer rushed down the path each morning to check her mailbox, going back instead to her normal routine of dropping the car window and leaning out to collect any post.

So it was as she was flipping through the bundle on her lap, discarding all the trash, that she suddenly realized that the letter before her was different.

Feverishly she tore it open. It began:

'Dear Jean,
   I'm so sorry to hear that your engagement to Don has been called off.'

Selfishly, her eyes raced over the page, desperate for a mention of the only thing she wanted to hear about. For the moment all the rest of the news could wait.

Then the word 'Adam' leapt out at her on the second sheet. She began to read, found the disappointment welling up in her as she took in the meaning.

'Adam hasn't been around to the hotel since that night. I only managed to go over to the teashop yesterday, but he wasn't there either, so eventually I asked — I hope that was all right?

They said he had gone away — somewhere. One of the women said they had heard he had been terribly upset at what had happened at the hotel. She thought it was the embarrassment, him being the Laird's son and all that.'

Jean felt a pain in her chest. She *had* hurt him then.

'Anyway, whatever the reason, he wasn't expected back for some time. So Jean, I took it on my head to try and get an address for him. I won't bore you with the details but I used a friend in the hotel's computer and business centre, and she faxed the estate office or something and found that he was in Glasgow. He went there the night you left, apparently, and never came back. The talk now is that Inverdee might not see him again. Whether that means he's ill or he's starting a new life or not, I have no idea; it's all a bit of a mystery.'

Jean feverishly searched for the Glasgow address, but it wasn't there. Bitterly disappointed she sat back, engine still running, and tried to grapple with what it all meant. She was excited — obviously she hadn't been just any other woman as far as Adam was concerned; she had, by all accounts, had a pretty devastating effect on him. But it was as much an enigma as before. Was he heartbroken — or just humiliated?

But one thing was now for sure: she knew that she would have to ask Kath to get the Glasgow address, would have to write and place herself at his mercy.

Whatever the consequences, she wanted Adam Crawford to know that he had won, that she truly loved him even if he did not her, and might cruelly use her to regain his own self esteem. It was a risk that she didn't care about any more. Suddenly, what she had to do was very clear.

Jean commenced reading the letter properly, and took great pleasure from the warmth of Kath's prose, the little pictures she drew in words of Inverdee and the people, and the goings on. Kath's concern at the cancellation of the marriage, and the fact that she wouldn't soon be seeing her friend after all was clearly genuine, and felt by Jean as well.

With the plea for the address would go

money for the ticket — taken from her own savings account. Jean wanted to see Kath, needed her support and friendship just at the moment, more than anything. There was no one else of her own age she could confide in.

Feeling better than she had for days she drove off to the hospital, totally unaware of the Ford station wagon parked at the kerb a hundred yards away.

A big man got out of the borrowed car when she had disappeared from sight, and made for the front door.

Don still had his key to the house . . .

12

To Jean, the day just seemed to fly past. There was a lightness about her step and manner, which others remarked upon. With the arrival of the letter and then her decision, it was as if an abscess had been incised and drained.

At the end of her shift Jean stopped by the travel agent, made arrangements and paid for a plane ticket collectable at any time at Glasgow airport. All Kath would have to do would be to check in at the airline desk a little earlier on the day of travel to claim the ticket.

Happily, she carried on to the hairdresser. She had phoned for an appointment earlier that day. An hour later, with it washed and trimmed, she bought some groceries and stopped by Mrs O'Neil to tell her what had happened.

The white-haired old lady listened as Jean read aloud the letter, all the time beaming with pleasure.

'I'm so happy for you, Jean. I wish you all the luck in the world. Now, won't you have something to eat? We're just about to have supper.'

With a genuine appetite for the first time in

weeks Jean accepted the invitation and was soon tucking into a plate piled high with delicious home cooking.

It was dark when she returned home, the headlights of the car sweeping past the lifeless windows of the house as she turned up the short drive and stopped in front of the garage.

Inside, she flicked on the lights in rotation as she made her way to the kitchen. It was as she was pouring milk into a glass that her eye suddenly caught the coffee cup and remains of a meal on the breakfast bar. Rooted to the spot, she looked down at it, for a second not comprehending, since she never ate cooked breakfast, knew it was not hers.

Then realization came, and the hair on her head prickled with fear. Don — he must have been there. The thought was overtaken by the ultimate one: was he still there now, inside the house?

She wheeled round, rushed into the lounge, clicking on lights. It took a second for it to register, but nobody was there. Jean made for the bedroom, threw open the door, tense with fear. It was pitch black inside. She snatched at the light switch. When the room was illuminated her eyes fell on a rumpled bed and finally, with an intake of breath, to the dressing table mirror. Written in her own

183

lipstick were the words, '*I haven't forgotten you, honey — you're still MY girl.*'

Jean backed out of the room, returned to the kitchen, frightened to the point of feeling sick.

But she was also angry.

For a long time she sat turning over in her mind what she could do. Don was going to continue to make trouble, that was for sure. It shocked her to think that she had been that close to marrying somebody she really hadn't the first idea about. She could go and live in the nurses' quarters, but that would mean giving in to him and that rankled.

Then she had an idea. If Kath would come immediately and stay a while, it would solve everything. Maybe afterwards she would leave — Wichita Falls was no longer a place she wanted to live in; it contained only memories, and a man she no longer wanted anything to do with.

She had no hesitation in reaching for the phone. The world was a smaller place, she realized, as the double ring tone of the British phone told her she was through.

'Hello?'

Jean felt a rush of sheer joy and relief.

'Kath, it's Jean.'

For a couple of minutes they were all over each other, laughing and giggling like a couple of teenagers. Finally Jean said, 'Kath — about Adam . . . ?'

Her friend's voice grew conspiratorial.

'Apparently he's staying at a hotel in Glasgow. I've got the address — and phone number. It's near the airport.'

Jean's heart missed a beat. He'd stayed there, then, since the day she had flown away!

Kath continued, 'Is that why you rang? I'll get it for you.'

Jean stopped her. 'No — no, it's not just that. Kath, at Glasgow airport there's a ticket waiting for you.' She explained what was happening to her, ending with a plea, 'I need company, Kath. I wondered if you'd come over at the end of the week — stay as long as you like. I know it's short notice but I'm a bit worried. I don't know what he'll do next.'

If she had any qualms that Kath would raise objections about her job, they were instantly dispelled.

'Oh Jean, of course I'll come. Are you sure you'll be all right till I can get there?'

Relieved, Jean said she would manage somehow.

Kath gave the details of her intended flight and Jean promised to be there to meet the plane on its arrival. Then, after a prolonged and reluctant farewell, she concluded, 'Kath,

I'm at my wits' end over this. You really are special.'

Kath said, 'Jean, take care now, and don't do anything foolish.'

They finally rang off. Jean felt lonely and vulnerable as she bolted the front door and checked all the windows. She would get the locks changed tomorrow.

★   ★   ★

It seemed a long time to the day of Kath's arrival. Jean was anxious each time she entered the house until the locksmith came.

By Friday evening, though, her spirits were high. So when the phone rang her heart fell. She just knew it was Kath. There must have been a hitch.

Fearfully, she answered, 'Hello?'

There was a delay before a man said, 'Is that you, Jean?'

There was no mistaking that voice, even though it came from a country thousands of miles away, travelling into space to a satellite and back to earth again.

The shock was so great she almost slammed the receiver down.

Was she going mad — having delusions?

The voice was low, gentle, pleading.

186

'Jean, don't hang up on me — just listen — '

Initially, in a daze, Jean did as she was told as Adam's voice dropped even lower.

'I've been through hell these past couple of weeks . . . You're the only woman I've ever — '

When there was so much she wanted to say, to ask, it staggered Jean to hear herself interrupt, question him in a strained, snappy voice.

'How did you get this number?'

He sounded miserable, deflated. 'I asked the tour people you came with. I made up an excuse.'

A flood of relief swept through her.

So Kath *hadn't* been in touch with him on her behalf; he'd done it all himself.

She relented a little, but was still puzzled as to why she wasn't all over him. Was there some basic female trait, some instinct borne of primeval femaleness that made her hold back? That as a man he had to prove himself worthy of her even though she was yearning, aching for him?

Her voice softened a little.

'It hasn't been very good for me either.'

'No? Then I'm sorry, Jean, believe me. I'll come straight to the point. I want to beg you — can we get back together again?'

Her heart missed a beat, but could it be true? Was he being genuine or . . . ?

As if he knew it was now that he had to convince her, he added quickly, 'I admit that I hadn't initially intended for us to be serious — I've been, well, coming over to the hotel for a long time, enjoying myself — '

She butted in, accusingly, 'A holiday affair — that was what I was going to be, wasn't it?'

He sounded wretched. 'Yes, that's what I thought, but when it happened I had no idea why I went off the rails — was an absolute bastard. It was only later when I'd had time to think, to sort things out in my head, that I realized it was *because* I was in love with you. The thought that it was your first time — and I could have been anybody . . . In some perverse way I blamed you for my own guilt, but Jean, believe me, it was all so quick, I couldn't cope. Then, when we made up I couldn't believe my luck, couldn't believe what had happened. I was just happy to thank God.

'What followed was the biggest shock of my life. It's only since then that I've realized who you are — the significance of it all.'

She whispered, 'Yes.'

Adam continued, 'I understand how you must have felt but that's all ancient history to me, so much so that I'm prepared to leave

Inverdee, leave Scotland for good. I'll sell everything, live anywhere in the world, do anything it takes' — his voice softened, pleaded — 'as long as I have you.'

Jean felt the tears flooding down her cheeks. Glad that he couldn't see her. She said,

'Adam, it wasn't all your fault. I acted like a silly young girl, and for that I apologize.'

There was a pause, and then he said,

'So there is a chance for us then?'

She nodded, and then foolishly realized he couldn't see her and whispered, 'Yes.'

She thought of all the things she wanted to say, all the things she had written down in the letter to him that was lying in the bureau.

She longed to reach out and touch him, to feel the hardness of his body and the softness of his hair, to taste the mouth that she sensed was so close, and yet was so far away.

He went on. 'Jean, I've written a long letter to you. I've put in it all the things I've thought about these past few weeks — about us, about our life together.' His voice said more shyly, 'I was going to send it to you when I found the courage — I didn't know when that would be. Now that I've spoken to you, may I send it?'

It was so incredible. In her misery she had done the same thing. She couldn't help but notice that it was so like one of her favourite Victorian novels.

Her voice was husky as she said, 'Adam — I've done the same.'

She blushed. 'Kath from the hotel is catching the morning flight out to Dallas. I'm meeting her. If you like you could give it to her?'

'I'd like that very much — lucky Kath. I'm dying to see you again.'

'Me too. I want — '

She stopped, was too embarrassed to say that she wanted to feel his strong arms around her; to feel safe, secure from all her present problems.

' — I want to ask, do you truly forgive me for what I did?'

His voice tensed. 'You mean, throwing my clothes out for all the world to find next morning?'

'I meant leaving you like I did . . . without any explanation. I was so foolish.'

He chuckled, a warm, beautiful sound that made her feel she was floating on air.

'Leaving me? I deserved everything I got. But as for throwing my clothes out of the window — never! I'll get you for that.'

She giggled, and said, 'Oh yeah?'

For the first time in their stormy relationship there was time for humour, time to step back from the overpowering raw emotion of their first encounters, to see more of their true selves.

Finally, Jean said in a very small voice, 'Adam, I do love you — you know that, don't you?'

Even over the phone she heard him swallow, then he said softly, with difficulty, 'You don't know how wonderful it is to hear you say that. I'll give my letter to Kath. Maybe after you've read it you'll think I'm a real softy — but I'll risk that. Everything I've written down, most of it in the wee small hours of the morning, is true. It adds up to one thing: I can't live without you.'

'I love you too.'

It didn't seem enough.

Though neither wanted to put the phone down, the last few minutes of their new beginning seemed to drain both of them.

Adam finally said, 'I'll call again after you've had time to read my letter.'

Jean answered softly, 'I'll be waiting.'

Afterwards, she sat there for ages, unmoving, the tears streaming down her face.

13

Jean worked the next day in a dream — had to keep pinching herself. Had it really happened?

Had Adam really phoned her? Or was she hallucinating — going mad? It was so marvellous she dared hardly believe it.

She finally went shopping at the local supermarket and grew more and more excited as she found herself buying for two — Kath would be with her next day.

It was gone seven o'clock and the shadows were lengthening by the time she turned the car into her avenue and drew near the house. It was then that she saw him, a shadow that moved, coming around the side of the house, stopping to look through a window and then jumping onto the porch and hammering on the door.

It was Don, his face black with fury.

For a split second Jean thought of driving on, of coming back later. Then she fisted the rim of the wheel in frustration. She knew this would happen sometime — so why start running away now?

She drew into the drive as he whirled

around and came striding towards her.

Jean stayed in the car, but wound down the window.

He rested his hands on the side and glared in at her.

'What the hell do you think you're doing?' he raged.

'I beg your pardon?'

He gestured at the front door, bellowed in at her, only inches from her face.

'You've changed the locks!'

Staring straight ahead Jean sat with her arms rigid, knuckles white on the wheel, chest heaving with the difficulty of breathing, so frightened was she of his physical presence.

She heard a little squeaky voice say, 'Why shouldn't I? It's nothing to do with you any more. I've told you, we're *through*.'

Instead of backing off he became more menacing, ripping the door open and ordering, 'Get out and open that door! We'll settle this inside.'

Jean stayed where she was, her legs trembling with fear. She knew that if she did as she was being bullied into, inside the house he would have her at his mercy.

Somewhere, born out of the realization that the little squeaky, terror-stricken voice that had said, 'Why shouldn't I?' was hers, and that it was just what a bullying coward of a man like Don and all the others who abused women expected, a sense of rage overcame her.

As a nurse in these troubled times they had all received instruction on what to do if attacked. They had been told that possibly the single most damaging belief held by women is that they were the weaker sex, and in so doing wore a subconscious air of submissiveness that attackers depended upon, for that was a prerequisite to the thing that most turned them on. How often had the term 'being in control' featured in a rapist's confession?

Jean let out a huge shout: 'No! Get away from me or I'll call the police!'

With that she hit the car horn and held it down. The continuous noise cut through the quiet street like a factory hooter. Startled, Don took a step back, and snarled, 'Cut that out, you stupid bitch!'

He made one more attempt to get at her, his hand reaching in and clamping on her nearest wrist, the other trying to prize her thumb from the horn.

He yanked it back, there was a violent stab of pain and it felt as if it was broken.

But Jean's other hand had already reached into the shopping bag beside her; desperately searching for what she knew was on top: a can of hair lacquer.

As soon as he yanked her hand off the wheel she managed to break it free, and bring it across to join the other, holding the can. For a fleeting moment of pure terror as he loomed in and reached for her, she found her thumb was useless, could not get the cover off the can. He had her around the shoulders, was roaring like a bull elephant and was lifting her bodily from the seat and out of the car when she got the lid off with her snatching fingers and depressed the nozzle.

The spray went straight into his eyes.

Instantly, Don let go of her, staggering back, hands clutching at his face, screaming like a kid,

'My God — you've blinded me. You bitch, what was that?'

Jean's legs refused to hold her up. She dropped heavily onto her knees on the tarmac, slumped forward onto her hands.

'Bleach!' she screamed at the ground, hoping that would demoralize him still further. It did. Don cried out wildly, staggered blindly across the lawn, trampling over the flower beds to his car.

He got in, fumbled with something in the front seat. It was then that she realized it was cans of beer; he'd probably been drinking all evening.

He snapped one open and poured the fluid over his upturned face. She knew it would be only a matter of seconds before he could see again.

Then she would be at great risk.

She grabbed her purse from the ground beside her, got up then fell again as her ankle turned and a shoe flew off. Limping, she got to the front door. Her hand was shaking so much the key wouldn't fit. She bit her lip, glanced over her shoulder. Her heart stopped. Don was lurching away from the car, coming towards her.

She turned back, dropped her purse, and held the key with two hands. Metal did a dance against metal, a sort of Morse code that was finally silenced as the key slid in. With a quick turn she opened the door, heard his heavy breathing as he lunged out, grabbing for her.

The door was barely closed when his full weight crashed into it.

Rigid with fear she forced her back against it as it quivered on its hinges as he hammered and kicked, all the while shouting a stream of profanity at her.

It was some time before it all went quiet. She stayed where she was. If he tried anything else, breaking a window, for example, she would instantly call the police, but knew that if she did so now, it would just be treated as a 'domestic', and in any case he had a lot of sympathetic buddies on the force. When Kath was there she guessed it would blow over. Don would get the message in the end.

It remained quiet for a long time before she heard his car start up.

She moved to a window, pulled aside the net and watched him drive away.

It was only then that she noticed her thumb. The pain felt as if it was pulsating in time with her heartbeat.

There was no doubt that she needed medical attention, but she couldn't face the thought of leaving the house unattended for a second time that night.

In the bathroom first aid box she found some bandage. With difficulty she bound the thumb against the palm. It would do until morning.

Morning! Next day! Kath would be there, arriving at Dallas, Fort Worth at six o'clock in the evening.

And with her would be Adam's letter.

Jean forgot all the unpleasantness, all the worry, everything, as she remembered again his voice, what he had said in that all too brief phone call that even now she was struggling to remember in detail.

Did he say he loved her?

Yes — yes she could remember *that*.

But she kept doubting herself. Had it really happened?

Well, tomorrow would bring the proof.

She began to worry that Kath wouldn't know what she was talking about, asking 'What letter?'

Maybe Adam wouldn't be able to contact her in time. But then, surely, he would call right away?

And if there was no letter, and no call — what then? The agony followed by ecstasy, followed by agony went on into the early hours of the morning before she finally dropped off into an uneasy sleep on a temporary bed she'd made up in the bathroom. It was just a precaution in case Don did something reckless. He wouldn't know where she was and, in any case, the door had the only bolt inside the house. She kept a house phone beside her.

But despite everything, her mind was on one thing only:

The letter.

14

Jean awoke with a start; momentarily thinking a noise had been responsible. But it was the sunlight streaming in through the glazed bathroom window and falling on her face.

She stretched, noticed her bandaged hand and drew it down for a closer inspection. Although it was sore to touch, the first-aid splint seemed to be working. It was no longer on fire as it had been the night before.

With a little difficulty she dressed, pulling on the jeans and top she had been wearing before she went to bed.

There was work to do around the house and, in any case, plenty of time for a bath and to get into something decent to meet Kath later on.

She freshened up, then unbolted the bathroom door and swung it open, intent on getting coffee and English muffins for breakfast. She pulled up with a scream as a figure lunged through an opposite door at her. Jean fell sideways, leaning for support on the doorframe, one hand on her thumping chest. Her heart seemed intent on banging itself free from its surroundings.

She'd completely forgotten the long, full-length mirror opposite. It was her reflection that had given her such a fright!

Out loud she took herself to task.

'For heaven's sake, woman, pull yourself together!'

She giggled as she realized that involuntarily she had used a pompous, manly voice. There were a lot of them like that, who still looked upon women as somehow inadequate; inadequate — and to be used. She shivered at the memory of the man she had thought she had known.

But then there were the others — like Adam Crawford. She longed for the hundredth time to have a photograph of him — mad with herself for not asking him to give one to Kath — even if it was only one of those awful instant things you got in booths for passports. *Anything.*

But surely there was no danger that she would — could — forget that beautiful masculine face as it had appeared above her, moving down to envelope her mouth in his, as sensations beyond anything she had ever experienced had possessed her — body and soul.

By the middle of the afternoon Jean's excitement at seeing Kath again had reached a peak of expectancy.

In trying not to be too early she had, typically, almost left it too late. She showered swiftly, dried even faster and in her underwear sat at the dressing table and started to quickly fix her face.

It was then that something strange happened — or rather, *seemed* to happen. It was almost as if somebody else was sitting there, guiding her hand.

Jean shook her head, tried to clear it, knew that all the fuss with Don was probably getting to her.

She carried on putting on her eye make-up — then suddenly sat back, frowning.

Her eyes looked different — set deeper than she usually had them — especially for a mid-afternoon.

Still puzzled, she nevertheless shrugged and carried on, setting the finishing touches to her cheeks and lips.

Jean reached out and found herself selecting a dark lipstick, one that she normally used on special evening occasions. Mystified, she looked at her finished face; a face she had last seen in Inverdee on the eve of the Highland Ball!

She remembered the feeling she had had then, a weird, but strangely not a frightening sensation that someone else was with her; *in* her; *was* her.

She shook her head, shivered as her back felt cold and got up and opened the closet door, at the same time pulling off her wrap and letting it fall to the floor.

She had intended to wear a short, sassy pinstripe suit so that Kath would be impressed with her all-American girl image, but as her hand went out to take it from the rack it seemed to veer to one side, and instead took hold of a hanger where she knew were hanging clothes she had never worn — clothes that had been intended for her honeymoon. It was a dress.

She pulled it off the rack, and held it up in front of her, pinning it with one hand to her hip as she swayed from side to side to make it flow over her body.

It was pure silk, with a draped cowl neckline, the bodice gathering to the waist and cinched with a matching belt. The bias-cut skirt was full and fluid, and passed over her extended leg like a green mountain stream. Against her reddish hair it was a very romantic dress.

Jean slipped it over her head and let it fall down over her outstretched figure. As it did so she seemed to be enveloped in a sea of green light — and something more . . .

A sensation of . . . timelessness, a serene expectancy? With the dress finally zipped up she took another look at herself with a pair of matching sling-back shoes.

Jean *felt* different — felt somehow calmer after all the troubles of the last few days with Don. It almost seemed as if she were floating on air as she tidied up her things, took a last look into the room she had prepared for Kath and then left the house for the journey to Dallas.

On the outskirts of Wichita Falls she had the gas tank filled and the screen washed, conscious of the looks the attendant gave her.

It was dusk by the time the tall ultra-modern skyscrapers of Dallas appeared in the distance, the red globe of the setting sun reflecting back off the dark, all-glass side of one of them so brightly it was as if there were two suns in the solar system.

It added to the dream-like feeling she had had in the last few hours, a feeling that she was on the verge of . . . what?

She frowned as she waited to negotiate a busy crossing. The red traffic light changed to green.

As she let the automatic engage and moved forward and she turned right, away from the city centre towards the airport, it came to her what she was experiencing.

She was moving away from the past, towards the future.

Adam was the future.

But all such beautiful thoughts had to be put aside as for the next half an hour she had to cope with the airport approach, the parking of the car, the walk to the entry port from which Kath would appear as if by magic — a wonder of this modern world they all took for granted.

Jean waited by the barrier with the rest of the crowd.

According to the television monitor the flight had landed. Every now and then the automatic doors leading out of the customs hall swished open, offering glimpses of people with their baggage at inspection tables. She could not see Kath.

Some one hundred people must have come through, and a dreadful disappointment was beginning to take hold when something occurred that made Jean stop breathing.

A ripple of light passed over her senses; the noisy concourse faded into the background. The unbelievable was happening. In the deep silence a voice in her head whispered, 'I told you so.'

All of a sudden Jean knew it was what she had been unconsciously hoping — praying — for during the last twenty-four hours; the reason why she had been so mysteriously 'possessed'.

As he saw her, his face lit up. But she was immobile, rooted to the spot, still unable to believe what was taking place.

He looked absolutely stupendous, towering over the others around him as he came towards her.

It was Adam.

15

He was wearing a white sports top with short sleeves, the muscles of his folded back arm which held a casual bag over his shoulder, bulging with athletic strength and power.

The open neck below the dimpled chin gave a breathtaking glimpse of the tangled hair that lay beneath. His jeans were well cut, but failed to disguise the strong, well-defined thighs that brought him towards her, even faster, his arm unhooking as he dropped his bag to the floor when he reached her.

For a split second he looked down at her with those blue eyes under dark hair and then together they reached out for each other.

Jean felt his arms wrap around her, overlapping behind her waist as she was lifted effortlessly from the floor, her own hands reaching up around his neck and twisting into the rich thickness of black hair as he swung her round and round.

He held her like that, their faces so close that his sweet breath was hot upon her lips, held so tantalizingly close to his own.

'Jean.'

It was all he could manage. Their lips met.

He had never been so gentle with her, a kiss that was a mere brush upon the lips, soon to be overtaken by his cheek pressing against hers as he murmured into her ear, 'You've no idea how I've longed for this moment.'

She realized her cheeks were wet, and then knew it wasn't just from her tears. Adam, her big, strong Highlander, was as overcome as she. Jean hung onto his broad shoulders, then, still held in the air, she drew her head free, cupped his face in her hands, gave it a long, searching look and then gave him an equally long, fierce kiss. Somebody going past wolf-whistled, but they paid no attention.

When finally she let go and pulled back she said, 'This is incredible. I can't believe you're here — you never said — '

Adam sounded anxious. 'Kath — she told me something that worried me.'

Guiltily, Jean suddenly remembered her friend, half turned, still in his arms, looking for her.

'Is she here?'

'No.'

Gently he lowered her to the ground.

'The flight was full so she gave me her seat.'

'But why?' Jean immediately regretted saying it — it sounded as if she wasn't pleased to see him when it was the most miraculous thing that ever could have happened.

Hurriedly she added, 'I mean, she was looking forward so much to coming.'

He looked at her intently.

'Jean, she said you were *scared*. Something about your ex-fiancé terrorizing you. I was beside myself with worry.' His hands rested lightly on her hips as though he wasn't going to let her go — not that she was trying to break free — as he asked softly, 'Is that true?'

Jean winced and nodded. 'He's been a bit silly. Nothing more, I promise. But I was looking forward to Kath's company.'

'Oh.' He looked crestfallen.

Jean placed her hands on his chest, slipped one just inside his shirt and ran her fingers through the hair.

'Kath's a good friend, but first things first.'

With that she stood on tiptoe and kissed him again.

'I still can't believe it — this is so wonderful,' she breathed.

'Jean.' He sounded anxious. 'You really have forgiven me?'

She shook her head. 'It's not for me to forgive you after what I did.'

Her free hand reached up to lightly brush the dimple in his chin. She felt the bristles as she asked softly, 'Have you forgiven *me*?'

His arms came around her, pulled her into him in a bear hug. They said nothing more, but for the first time in days she felt completely safe — a warm feeling of being where she belonged — of being *his*.

Finally, still with one arm around her, he picked up his bag.

'Come on, let's get out of here.'

They walked to the car. He slung his bag onto the back seat as she fired up the engine.

He saw it for the first time when she put her hands on the steering wheel.

'What have you done to your thumb?'

She tried to play it down.

'I was doing something — it was an accident.'

'Him? Don?' His voice was like ice.

'Well . . . yes, but — '

'Tell me.'

There was no refusing him. It was said with such cold finality that she shivered with the stark revelation of the other side of his nature — a man as a primeval savage — and yet at the same time it gave her a strong instinctive sense of being secure, protected.

She told him.

When she'd finished she glanced across, fearful of his reaction. But he just said, very quietly, 'I see', and said no more, staring straight ahead.

In an irrational way, it disappointed her. Momentarily the conversation lapsed. He continued to just stare out of the window.

Jean decided to change the subject, make small talk. Whilst she was driving it was impossible to say all the other things she wanted to say. Even so, hearing herself ask, 'Is this your first visit to America?' seemed very banal.

To her relief he finally chuckled.

'No — but I've never been down this way.'

They talked some more as she worked her way out of Dallas and finally settled down for the long, steady journey home.

It was dark, and the traffic began to dwindle. After a while it seemed a good time, cocooned in their own little world, to bring up the thing that most worried her.

'What about your family, Adam? What will they say about you seeing a . . . a Johnson?'

He stretched back in his seat, crossed his long legs and put his hands behind his head.

'Well now, I've got something here that will take care of that.'

Puzzled, she asked, without taking her eyes off the road,

'What?'

He murmured, 'Wait and see.'

Bemused, she said no more. She knew already that if Adam had made up his mind it would be revealed later, then that was an end to it.

The long drive home was made longer by a detour. The steady drone of the car engine was a backdrop to their occasional talk. Jean found driving at night required all her attention, and it had started to rain slightly.

'Would you like some music?' she asked.

Adam grunted and yawned, his out-stretched arm lying protectively across her shoulder.

'Mmm — that would be nice. Something low and romantic.'

Jean felt really good; his arm was so comforting, just keeping in contact, laying a claim to her that was affectionate without being overly possessive. It was beyond belief. Was it really happening?

The low sound of a trio, piano, sax and bass murmured in the background as mile after mile of road swept past. His hand came to rest on her shoulder even more heavily.

When the lights of an oncoming car lit the interior she glanced across at him.

He was asleep. With her attention back on the road she smiled in the returned darkness.

Poor dear. It had all been too much for him — he was exhausted. She knew that he hadn't slept on the plane, or the night before, worrying that he would miss Kath at the airport.

After what seemed a lifetime they arrived back at Wichita Falls, and finally to her house.

In the driveway it was strange seeing him there, stirring from his sleep, burying his face in his hands, rubbing his eyes. Through his fingers he said, 'I'm sorry, I feel absolutely bushed.'

She opened the door, and got out, grinning.

'Let's get you to bed — and I mean to *sleep*.'

She was still chuckling at the unintentional meaning when suddenly, out of the darkness came a figure.

Jean froze with horror. It was Don, and he was carrying a whip, the sort stockmen used on cattle. In his other hand was a whisky bottle.

He staggered over.

'There you are, you crazy little bitch. It's time you were taught a lesson.'

The dropped bottle smashed on the ground and Jean was grabbed before she could move.

He flung her face down on the car hood and drew back the whip.

It was only then that Don realized someone

else was there. A fist that felt like an iron shackle gripped his wrist and held the descending whip hand, frozen in mid-flight.

'What the hell?'

He half turned to find a face in his, a face that, if he had been born four centuries earlier and in a country far away, he would have realized was a clan chief, a warrior of supreme strength and courage.

But all he saw was long black hair and hooded, ice-blue eyes that spoke of death and destruction — *his*.

What followed left Jean feeling sick — but elated. With a short stab of a punch Adam hit Don in the stomach. She heard a grunt as she broke free, saw him doubled up, saw Adam twist the whip hand so that Don had to fall forward to avoid the pain of dislocation. The whip fell to the floor. Adam picked it up as he put a foot on the back of Don's neck, holding him down — choking.

The Scots accent was thicker, his voice so full of menace that Jean fleetingly felt sorry for Don.

'Jean's mine now. Come anywhere near my woman again and you're dead.'

With that Adam flung the whip away into the night.

'Do you get it, man?' To emphasize the point he trod even harder on Don's windpipe, then released the pressure altogether.

Choking, Don managed, 'Yeah — okay.'

Adam stood back, allowing him to get slowly to his feet.

Rubbing his neck, no mean size himself, Don glowered at his adversary, then as he moved past Jean he went to hit her. 'You f — '

He got no further.

Adam sprang like a panther. The fight was short and brutish, but the most frightening thing of all was the difference Jean saw in Adam. The look on his face was like nothing she had seen before.

Don finally held up his hands as he staggered back against the car and slid down on his haunches, bleeding from his nose and mouth, one eye almost closed.

'Okay. Okay — I get the message.'

Adam flicked his head.

'Get out of here. Next time you might get seriously hurt.'

They watched him stagger away. Voice hushed, Jean said, 'Where did you learn to do things like that?'

Adam's face gradually lost its mask. His eyes twinkled. 'Sauchiehall Street on a Saturday night.'

When he saw the puzzled look in her eyes he explained. 'It's in Glasgow, before I was a Queen's Own Highlander.'

He said nothing of his SAS training.

Jean started to shake, and leant against him. 'You probably saved my life.'

His arm came around her shoulders, squeezed her against him. 'Then I'm glad I came — for both our sakes.'

'He won't come back, will he?'

Adam smiled down at her.

'Don't you worry any more. I'm here now, and I'll never leave you.'

Trembling with shock Jean held tightly onto him, gathering strength from his rock-like presence.

Still holding her he reached down and picked up his bag.

'Now then, let's see this house of yours.'

Shaken, Jean opened the front door, and led the way into the hall. She pointed at the various doors.

'That's the kitchen, lounge there and that's the bathroom, and this — this is the master bedroom.'

She opened the door and falteringly went inside, feeling suddenly shy. The double bed seemed to fill the room.

'This was my parents'. You can sleep here; my bedroom is across the corridor.'

Jean felt terrible, saying it like that, especially after what he had just done for her, and added lamely, 'Like I said, you need a good night's sleep, I'm sure.'

He dropped his bag and put his arms around her, drew her to him again and gave her a wordless embrace, finally kissing the top of her head.

'You're right.'

He drew away and sat down heavily on the bed, grinning sheepishly from under those dark eyelids.

'I'll give you my letter — that will do for tonight. Read it when you're in bed.'

Jean blushed at the thought, found the idea of reading his words of passion while he slept only yards from her uncontrollably erotic.

Then she remembered something.

'Adam, in the car when I asked you how your side of the family would take to you being with me, a Johnson, you said you had something that would take care of that.'

His half-shut, come-to-bed eyes looked up at her.

'That's right.'

Puzzled, she watched as he reached into his pocket and brought out a small black box. Like any woman she knew what it was, what it must contain, her heart missing a beat as he opened it and handed it to her.

But she was completely unprepared for the ring that nestled in the old blue velvet.

Jean looked at it and back to him, speechless.

Softly he whispered, 'I want you to marry me, Jean — in Inverdee church. That's my grandmother's engagement ring; it's over two hundred years old. At last our families will be truly united — and nobody can do a damn thing about it.'

Tears welled up in her eyes. Still unable to say anything he asked again.

'Will you, Jean? Will you marry me?'

She finally nodded, and gave him the box back.

'Put it on my finger, Adam.'

He took the ring with its diamond set in old gold and held it up. It caught the light, flashing in her eyes.

Immediately a shiver ran through her, instantly recognizable as the same sort of feeling she had had several times recently — starting in Inverdee the night of the ball — and even this very night when she was choosing the dress she was wearing for Adam. And always a feeling of déjà vu.

But as he slid it onto her finger she suddenly knew what it was all about.

She felt the presence of the woman whose ring it had been, in another time, another place; felt her satisfaction that at last her son's son was doing the right thing. She had been watching over them from the moment Jean had arrived in Inverdee.

And as Jean gazed at the shimmering light coming from her finger she felt the other woman's presence fading.

She drew her hand and the ring to her breast and whispered to herself, to the other woman as she faded away. 'Thank you. I'll take good care of him.'

Adam's anxious voice sounded in her ear, brought her back to the world of now.

'Jean — are you all right?'

It was as herself that she sat on his lap and wrapped her arms over his wide shoulders.

'I love you, Adam Crawford.'

16

By mutual consent they did not sleep together, that was something both of them were resolved not to do until their wedding night.

But otherwise, they were as domesticated as two newly-weds could be.

She cooked a breakfast of scrambled eggs and hash browns as he showered, singing at the top of his voice, the Robert Burns song that had been sung on the night of the ball.

> *O my Love's like a red red rose*
> *That's newly sprung in June*
> *O my Love's like the melodie*
> *That's sweetly play'd in tune*
> *As fair art thou, my bonnie lass*
> *So deep in luv am I*
> *And I will luv thee still, my dear*
> *Till a' the seas gang dry.*

She liked that a lot and smiled happily to herself.

Afterwards she took him for a ride to the hospital, where she went in to see a woman in human resources and gave in her notice, saying she was getting married — hearing her voice saying it out loud to somebody was a thrill in itself — and would be quitting her job sooner rather than later.

After that she drove them to her favourite shopping mall for a coffee.

It continued to look and feel strange having him there with her, in all the old haunts; sad that her parents weren't alive to see them.

Jean was conscious of the many admiring looks he was getting from the little groups of women shopping and gossiping in Starbucks.

She felt pride, and not a little anxiety all at the same time, and ended up scolding herself for acting like a schoolgirl on a first date.

It was as they were getting back into the car, Adam mistakenly going to the wrong side, forgetting that steering wheels in American cars are on the left, that the first sighting happened.

He saw Don, just coming out of the mall.

Saying nothing to Jean he watched as the figure in blue jeans, cowboy boots and red check shirt, topped with a white western hat, seemingly oblivious to them, got into his pick-up and reversed out of the space, exiting the parking lot with a squeal of rubber.

It could have been a coincidence, the town wasn't all that big after all, but it was worrying to think that when he returned to

Scotland, Jean might well bump into Don.

It was unsettling.

That night Jean took him to her favourite restaurant, a little Italian garden place, with overhead vines and little table candles flickering in red glass containers on white tablecloths.

After they had ordered, she plucked up the courage to ask him something that had been nagging at her all day.

'Darling, your parents, what will they be thinking — you getting married so quickly to a girl they don't even know?'

He could see the worry in her eyes, and stretched out his hand to cover hers as he said, 'They live abroad at the moment. Father's a diplomat. But I can tell you for sure they will adore you, especially Mother. Always said we needed new blood in the line, and there's a great tradition of American lassies marrying into decrepit old families — Winston Churchill's mother is a good example.'

He chuckled at that. Jean smiled weakly, but persisted.

'That's different. I'm not wealthy, just a lowly working girl, and besides,' she paused, raised an eyebrow, 'I'm a Johnson, don't forget.'

Adam lifted her hand, the diamond of the

engagement ring shooting out rays of reflected red light from the flickering candle, and brought it to his lips.

His eyes were alive with mischief.

'My father did worse than that — he married an English lass.'

He chuckled, then added seriously, 'It's time all that rot ended — was forgotten. This is the twenty-first century — it's history. Besides, I want to make amends.'

'Oh darling.' Jean stood up, leaned across the table and gave him a quick kiss, conscious of not making a fuss in public. If they had been on their own she would have hugged and kissed him and never let him go.

Glad, now that she had brought up her worries, Jean enjoyed her meal of mushroom risotto, washed down a glass of Chianti as they made heady plans for the future, finally getting around to the awful fact that he would have to leave the day after tomorrow.

When he saw her face fall he tried to cheer her up.

'Darling, I came on impulse, just had to, I dropped everything. It's been bad enough since you left; I've neglected so much that I'm in all sorts of trouble with business associates and the estate people — took my eyes off the ball big time. But we'll be together soon — for always.'

Jean put on a brave face.

'You're right, I'm being selfish. I'm so thankful to you for what you did.'

They talked a lot more, then finally Adam called for the bill.

When he'd paid, they stood up, Jean leading the way past the other tables, the music from a man playing an accordion and dressed in traditional Italian Alpine gear and a feathered trilby, drifting over the other diners. Waiters in long white aprons were busy with trays of food and bottles of wine.

It had been the perfect place to have enjoyed their first proper date together.

And then something happened that would bring Jean crashing down to earth.

Across the street from the restaurant garden was a bar called Hogan's. Through the open double doors came loud music from a jukebox and the rattle of coin machines above the constant background noise of pool-playing men and screaming women.

A large crowd of youths stood out front gathered around small tables, smoking and drinking. One group was particularly rowdy, grouped around and among a stand of Harley Davidson motorbikes.

Jean held tightly onto Adam's hand as they turned away, walking to her car parked further up the street.

'We get a lot of young motorcycle riders in the ER, showing off to their buddies after a few drinks, sometimes with tragic results.'

They got into the car. Jean started the engine, checked her mirrors and pulled away from the kerb.

As they drove past Hogan's, Adam suddenly found himself catching sight of a face in the crowd that he recognized. It was Don.

Again, maybe that was something he might have dismissed as yet another coincidence, but when, some minutes later, half a dozen motorbikes roared up behind them, flashing their lights, some driving alongside, swearing and giving the finger, and yee-hawing like cowboys, he knew that it wasn't.

He couldn't see Don. Some had helmets and large goggles, so he could have been one of them, but it didn't matter.

The incident lasted some two minutes, no more, and then they all roared away as a police cruiser passed in the other direction.

Jean let out a 'Phew', and glanced across at him.

'Just as I said, boys showing off. What must you think of the place.'

Adam lied.

'Same the world over.'

But he knew that it had not been just

youthful exuberance and misbehaviour.

They drove on in silence, the earlier magic of the evening for the moment, destroyed.

It became even more sombre as, once in the house, he began checking out of the windows to see that the street was empty.

Jean frowned and looked anxiously at him, sensing his answer even before he said it.

'What are you doing?'

Grimly he turned back to her.

'Jean, that incident with the motorbikes, there was more to it than that. Don was with that group. I saw him outside the bar.'

Her face crumpled.

'Oh God.'

Jean looked so frightened that he took her into his arms, stroked her sweet-smelling hair and comforted her as he would a child before kissing the top of her head. Then gently set her away from him as he said firmly, 'Enough is enough. He's clearly going to keep on giving you grief while you are still here. I think he's mental, myself.'

Holding her firmly by the shoulders now, Adam confronted her.

'Seriously, is there any reason why you can't just pack your bags and come back with me right now? You can stay at our house, have your own room. Our housekeeper Mrs

McElland will take care of you until the wedding.'

Seeing her hesitate he went on hurriedly, 'Or we could put you up at the hotel.'

Jean, still shaken, tried to think straight, and came to the conclusion that no, there was no good reason why she couldn't leave right away.

And the thought of Adam gone, of being alone again with Don still around, was terrifying.

She searched his face, wanting to be sure.

'Do you really mean it?'

'I've never been so sure of anything in my life before. I don't want you here, so far from me.'

Jean leant into him with relief.

'Oh darling, thank you.'

He kissed her again, then said, 'I'll get onto the airline immediately, get you a ticket.'

Half an hour later, they began packing.

In two big cases she put everything that mattered most to her, starting with all the framed photographs on various tables, and the photograph albums from the book-shelves. Then she swept up anything with sentimental value from her childhood, including the old lead and bowl of her long-dead Spaniel Bertie, an item or two from college days, a small picture off the wall and two other larger ones taken from their frames and some nursing certificates.

She also threw in some favourite pieces of cutlery her mother liked, and bubble wrapped two mugs with Pa's and Ma's written on them, a souvenir of the last vacation they had all taken together to Florida a couple of years back. She had already put in some things from her mother's dressing table.

The rest had been her clothes, some favourite pieces and some sentimental ones, like her first proper fashionable coat that she had bought with her first month's wage packet, which she hardly wore now, but meant a lot to her. It was part of her history, who she was.

Just before Adam sat on the larger case to get it shut she squealed with horror, rushed away and came back with a sports jacket that had belonged to her father, and a silk dress of her mother's.

She held the latter to her face, breathing in its still-lingering scent.

Adam shook his head.

'You won't get them in this one. Have you got another case, or something will have to come out?'

But Jean wouldn't budge. In the end they piled the clothes into two big black garbage bags, together with some trinkets from the mantelpiece, with a view to buying a third case on the way, or at the airport.

Resignedly he shook his head.

'We're going to have to pay a lot of excess weight.'

Mortified, Jean said, 'I'm sorry, I'll take care of it.'

Adam looked up at her from the case he was sitting on.

'Darling, this is your life, it's got to be done. I'm not complaining. A month or two from now, when you've sold the house, we'll get every last thing sent over by ship container — everything — all the furniture, *everything*. I want you to be happy.'

Thrilled, not sure if he really meant it, Jean asked, 'Where would we put it all?'

'In our first house — a cottage on the estate.'

At that, she came and sat on his lap, put her arms around his neck and kissed him.

'I don't deserve you, I love you so much.'

Adam was firm.

'No, it's *me* that doesn't deserve *you*, and I love you more than I can say.'

The next morning after breakfast, despite their weight Jean was impressed with the way Adam effortlessly put the cases into the car; her two in the trunk, and his smaller one on the back seat.

She took a last look around, tears appearing in her eyes.

'Goodbye, house.'

Gently, she closed the door, closing off the first part of her life. It was gone, forever. She had her memories, but now the future beckoned.

Using two cars, a new rental and her own, they went into town in convoy.

Jean met with her bank manager, then went straight around to a realtor with a set of keys and instructions to sell, and — Adam was insistent — orders for a removal and storage company with overseas experience to remove all the house contents either then or at the time of completion.

They left her car at a used auto dealer, with the bank's address to send the cheque to, though Jean knew it would be very modest.

They found a luggage store, bought another case and transferred the contents of the black bags into it, together with some things from one of the other cases, as there was a lot more room.

Now, Jean gazed out of the window as the houses of Wichita Falls went past, finally reaching the city limits, and the vast flat dusty plain of North Texas began to roll by, mile after mile, after mile.

It was so different from the Highlands, everything was so different. Her poor mother must have had a terrible shock. Yet her love for her father had never wavered.

Jean's stomach was tight with excitement and worry. Everything had happened so fast, so crazily fast.

She'd experienced a wonderful love, followed by crushing disappointment, then overwhelming happiness, swiftly followed by Don's frightening attitude.

On top of that, despite Adam's reassurances, she was still concerned about his parents and friends.

Would they look upon her as some little American gold-digger?

Adam checked the rear view mirror again as they drove along the 140 miles of Route 287 to Dallas. There was no sign of anything untoward, but though he hadn't said anything to her, he thought he'd seen Don's car just before they had joined the highway.

He grunted. Perhaps he was imagining things. There were, after all, thousands of that type of pick-up truck around.

But the colour had been the same.

At the airport they checked in, duly paid for the excess baggage, then after passing through security, found a little coffee area.

They ordered, then sat sipping, almost without speaking.

Adam looked at Jean's drawn, tired, but still beautiful face, and wondered at the spirit and the love she must have to uproot so completely, so suddenly, from everything she knew, and to go with him with such blinding trust. Adam knew this was the most extraordinary girl, and the fact she still wanted him, especially after his behaviour, was truly a miracle.

17

It was pouring with rain, and very dark when they arrived at Glasgow airport in the early morning.

As the plane's wheels made contact with the ground, from her window seat, by the lights of the runway, Jean could see spray enveloping the wings as the engines went into reverse thrust, braking them heavily until they came to a walking pace.

Then followed an interminable time as the big jet rumbled and juddered slowly back to the terminal building, and taxied up to the stand.

The engine noise began to die away. Everybody stood up in a rush; overhead lockers were opened.

Adam stayed where he was and said to her, 'Let's wait. Nobody is going anywhere for a while, and besides, you all end up waiting for your luggage at the baggage claim.'

It was another forty-five minutes — with Adam pushing a trolley piled high with their luggage — before they reached the automatic sliding doors of the exit.

Two exasperated customs officials had

finally given up searching through Jean's things. They marked the outside of the cases with white chalk crosses and then left a vexed Adam to shut them.

In the main concourse of Arrivals a crowd was waiting, some holding up notices with names written on them.

'Over here, sir.'

Adam's face lit up.

'Jean, this way.'

She saw a man walking quickly to the end of the roped-off section, calling out to them.

'Good to have you back, sir.'

He was in a heavy cream raincoat, with extra shoulder covers, and a Glengarry on his head. Everything was wet, including his face, but his grey eyes under heavy curling eyebrows and surrounded by weather-beaten cheeks, were twinkling with good humour.

When they reached each other the men shook hands, and then Adam introduced her.

'Jean, this is Angus McTavish, our estate manager. Angus this is Miss Jean Sinclair, my fiancée.'

Jean's hand was taken, surprisingly gently, by a calloused, working hand.

'I'm very pleased to meet you, Miss. Everybody is looking forward to seeing you at the house.'

Jean was only just beginning to realize that she didn't have any idea of Adam's wealth, not that it mattered in the least.

What mattered, was, he had said *fiancée*. It sounded wonderful.

The men talked, mostly about things and people to do with the estate as Jean sheltered under a large umbrella, held by Adam, until they reached a dark green Range Rover in the multi-storey car park.

There was no 'edge' with Adam, she was pleased to note. He helped Angus with the heavy luggage before opening a rear door for her.

'Do you mind, darling, if I sit in the front? I want to talk to Angus.'

'Of course not.'

Jean climbed up into the fine-smelling leather interior. It was all so different from the little car she had left at home — No, *this* was home now.

As they drove out of the covered car park they were hit by a squall of heavy rain, the windshield wipers leaping into a frenzy of activity.

She listened to Angus's deep Scottish voice as he said, 'Ay, it's been raining heavily nearly all night. Forecast is for it to dry up around lunchtime.'

Adam replied, saying something about a

shoot that had been arranged for the next day.

Their talk, and the streets awash with the driving rain, gridlocked cars and buses with headlights full on in the gloom of the morning rush hour, made her realize just what a leap into the unknown she had made. A vacation was one thing; a change of life was a very different matter.

But Jean looked back into the car, at the man sitting in front of her, with just the slightest sight of his face in profile as he half turned to speak to Angus, and knew she was in safe hands, that she had done the only thing that mattered in the world to her; she had followed her heart, not her head, thank God.

She trusted Adam implicitly.

And in any case, women made cultural changes in the name of love every day.

Love was the important thing. You could live anywhere in the world with it — and wherever it was, that was home.

They didn't go into Inverdee as she expected, but turned up a small lane some three miles out.

The rain had indeed stopped as Angus had said it would but they seemed to be in low cloud as the car steadily climbed past trees and hedges dripping with moisture.

Finally, the Range Rover slowed, its indicator warning light ticking on the dashboard, then they were turning through open wrought-iron gates flanked by old stone columns.

Adam craned around in his seat, and smiled at her.

'Darling, we're home.'

It was a short drive past clipped shrubs and beautifully mown lawns, then out of the mist loomed an old stone house, its Georgian entrance porch flanked on each side by two generous long windows that reached almost to the ground. Ivy grew up the walls to five smaller bedroom windows, and above them a row of even smaller dormer windows set in the blue slate tiles darkened by the rain.

On both sides of the main house were smaller wings, two storeys high.

With Angus this time holding the umbrella for her, she stepped out, surveying the beautiful door which then opened, and a small, grey-haired lady, dressed in a wraparound Dutch apron, came out into the covered porch.

'There you are, sir.'

Adam put his arm around the lady's shoulder and gave her a hug.

'Annie, this is Jean.'

Annie looked Jean up and down.

'Well now, Master Adam, your description didn't even begin to get anywhere near to describing how beautiful she is.'

Jean screwed her face up as she held out her hand. Adam continued, saying, 'Jean, this is Mrs McAllister — Annie to everybody. She's been looking after me on and off for more years than I can remember, ever since I was a little boy home from school, and Oxford even.'

They shook hands, Annie closing her other hand over Jean's and patting it as Jean said, 'Thank you for the compliment, but I must look a mess this morning after that red-eye flight.'

'Nonsense, lassie, at your age nothing matters. Now come in, come in, you'll catch your death of cold in this wet. I'm sure you must be hungry. I've got the kettle on and porridge and oatcakes if you wish, but it will be no trouble to make fried eggs and bacon.'

Adam, who had turned to help Angus with the luggage, called over his shoulder, 'Bacon and eggs for me, please, Annie, but first we need to freshen up. Give us half an hour; I could do with a shower. Do you mind showing Jean to her room?'

Annie took her by the elbow.

'Of course. You really meant her to be in

the green room? It's right down the end of the passage, you know? The poor wee lass will be lonely.'

Adam gave Jean a knowing smile and said firmly, 'Yes, Annie. Jean needs plenty of space and privacy to settle in. I don't want her to feel we're all on top of her — she's used to the wide open spaces of Texas, you know.'

Jean knew he was trying to make a joke out of it, because her little home was nothing like this magnificent country pile.

Gratefully, she nodded her thanks, then followed Annie across the dark oak-beamed and -floored hall, with a log fire burning in the big stone fireplace. Deers' heads with antlers looked down on the polished oak table in the middle of the hall, which was set with a large bowl of flowers.

It was all so beautiful.

She had to apologize to Annie, and say, 'Sorry, I missed that,' as the woman was talking all the time.

'I said, would you like a cup of tea while you freshen up — it will be no trouble.'

Jean reassured her.

'That's very kind of you — but no, I'll wait.'

They climbed a wide creaking staircase with its sweeping balustrade, ending in carved lions' heads top and bottom. Beneath her feet the old red carpet was held in place by long brass stair rods, and gave out onto a broad landing dotted with plinths and busts from antiquity, and jardinières with palms.

Leading the way, Annie turned up another, smaller staircase, carpeted in a modern beige material, the balustrade now painted a gloss white.

The next landing was smaller. Annie paused at the nearest door, opened it, and stood aside for her.

'Here we are, Miss. The bed is aired and I've put fresh towels in the bathroom.'

Jean walked into a room painted lime green, with matching floral curtains and the same material on the bed covers.

A door led into an en-suite shower room and W.C.

'Oh, it's beautiful.'

Jean looked around, then out of the window at a walled garden with gravel paths and a fountain.

'Well, if there's nothing else, Miss, I'll be away to the kitchen to get things ready.'

Jean thanked her. When she was gone she kicked off her shoes, flopped back onto the bed and looked up at the white ceiling.

The house was like a brilliant jewel set in these rolling hills and far-flung mountains, albeit the latter today shrouded in mist and cloud and only seen occasionally, like a lost fairyland. Everything was so far removed from the harsh burning and then alternatively freezing plains she had grown up with.

It was all so unbelievable, like being in a dream.

But people woke up from dreams, didn't they. Would it last, would she 'wake up'?

Maybe her mom and dad were looking down on her, taking care of her.

Further introspection was interrupted by a knock on the door.

Jean swung her legs to the floor, crossed to the door and opened it.

Angus stood there with her cases. She got him to put them both on her bed, saying apologetically, 'I'm sorry they're so heavy.'

In his lovely brogue, he said, 'No problem, Miss. If that's all I'll be on my way.'

She thanked him again, conscious that although he was very fit looking, he was no spring chicken. She closed the door.

Quickly she stripped off, tucked her hair under the shower cap provided and stepped into the cubicle.

With hot water streaming down her body Jean began to feel invigorated.

Adam had been as good as his word, giving her space, though the large house made it easier. Jean already felt at home in this very feminine room.

She presumed his room was on the main landing below.

She towelled briskly and then rummaged in one of the cases, taking out all sorts of things before she found fresh underwear. The customs people had left it in a mess.

And because she felt the dampness of the climate, summer or not, she opened a packet of pantyhose and pulled them on, followed by a woollen skirt and topped with a soft cashmere sweater with a roll neck.

She chuckled to herself as she attacked her hair. What on earth would she be wearing in winter? Her hair needed a wash — she wished she hadn't used a cap — but there hadn't been time to do it properly. She tied it back, before touching up her eyes and lips.

As soon as she opened the door, despite being at the top of the house, she could smell the frying bacon.

Jean tripped eagerly down to the hall, then followed her nose to a half-open door at the rear, down a small passage, and eased it open.

Before her was a large stone-flagged kitchen, dominated by a huge pine table and chairs down the middle.

Mrs McAllister was at a range, with a

battery of saucepans hanging to the right and left.

Adam, dark hair still damp, was already at the table, sipping a mug of coffee, morning newspaper spread out before him.

He caught sight of her and stood up.

'Everything all right?'

She pulled out a chair opposite him.

'Oh Adam, the room is beautiful.'

Relieved, he closed the paper.

'Glad you like it. I thought it was the best one for you.'

Intrigued, Jean was going to ask him why, but Mrs McAllister bustled over with two plates of egg, bacon and fried bread, and something called black pudding.

Jean asked what it was, and when she was told it was made with blood she couldn't stop herself from exclaiming, 'Ugh'.

Adam laughed, and teased.

'You'll be getting used to it, my lass, when you cook it for me.'

Before Jean, mock-serious, could advise him that changes would be made to his lifestyle, Angus came through an outside door, a very damp Gordon Setter bounding in after him. It went straight to Adam, who set down his knife and fork to ruffle the dog's ears and pat its back. Then, holding him down as he said, 'Steady, steady,

Monty, you're all wet.'

He looked over at Jean.

'This is Monty, my dog. Now, he's *our* dog.'

As if on cue, the dog left him and rushed around to thrust his snout straight onto her lap.

Laughing, she cupped his head in her hands and moved her face nearer.

'You're a lovely boy, aren't you.'

The dog's tail swished back and forth in excitement.

Adam chuckled.

'He likes you all right. Always goes for good-looking girls.'

She gave him a dismissive look, and then turned her attention back to Monty. When Mrs McAllister's back was turned, Monty enjoyed a nice slice of black pudding.

For Jean, it was the final, comforting welcome to her new home.

That night, she slept soundly.

For the next two days Adam showed her most of the estate. He let her drive the 4×4, at first down the rough forest tracks, and later sat beside her as she drove into Inverdee, on the wrong side of the road, as she put it. He showed her where to park, and they took coffee at little individual cafés, letting people get to know her, and her them, always with the introduction, 'This is my American fiancée, Jean.'

They walked Monty — there had always been a dog called Monty ever since Adam's grandfather had returned from the 8th Army in World War Two, named after the famous general that even Jean had heard of.

Adam took her to the stables, showed her his horse, Betsy, that she had first seen him riding, what seemed ages ago.

Adam patted Betsy, rubbed his hand affectionately up and down between her eyes as she snorted and pawed the ground with one hoof.

He looked back at Jean.

'Do you ride?'

She had spent all her life in Texas, but like most people who lived in towns she had only attended rodeos and the like as a spectator.

She shook her head.

'Afraid not.'

'Do you want to?'

Guardedly, Jean said, 'Well, if I'm to live here, and you do . . . '

Adam gave her a broad grin.

'You *are* going to live here, and that horse over there' — he pointed — 'is a nice quiet wee beastie to get started on.'

Jean's jaw dropped.

'I'm — I'm not dressed for — ' She saw the

twinkle in his eye. 'Oh, you swine.'

She hit him on the arm, and would have again but he grabbed her wrist, pulled her into him, and closed his mouth around hers as she tried to speak.

She only struggled, nominally, for a second, then abandoned herself to the heat of his mouth, his taste, his tongue, and the iron grip from which there was no escape — not that she tried again.

Later, in the Range Rover, driving back to the house, he stopped, pulling off onto an area of short grass that ended at a gate, with a dark forest beyond.

He didn't say a word as he got out, just walked around to her door, and opened it.

Tingling with expectancy, Jean knew what was coming.

He held out his hand, helped her down and held her close.

'Jean, I love you . . . '

She could see the torment in his eyes, put a finger to his lips.

Never taking her eyes from his, she took off the light coat she was wearing and spread it on the ground, and then sank down, holding out her hands for him to join her.

Adam swallowed, slowly lowered himself to be beside her then he rolled onto her.

This time his kiss was gentle, but as it

continued, she found the heat in her body rising, could not contain herself.

He was reluctant at first, but Jean took his hand to her heart. She felt her nipples hardening and willed him to slide it under her bra.

He did.

The elastic material flipped up; her breast fell free. His cupped hand took its weight, his thumb delicately stroking the very tip.

Jean could hardly contain herself, her one hand gripping the hair at the back of his head, her other tugging the shirt out from his trousers, then clawing at his bare back.

Breathing hard, he held her hair and pulled until her face was vertical, facing the sky, then his mouth came down on her neck. She could feel his teeth pressing into her skin.

Suddenly his hand left her breast, reached down, found her knee, moved up under her skirt, ruffling it as it went. Jean wanted him to go on, wanted to be consumed completely in the fire that was raging again in her body, like it had the night of the ball.

But when his hand reached her womanhood, as she convulsed with passion, as it went up her belly to the top of her pantyhose to pull them down, Adam suddenly let out a groan and let go, rolling off her.

They lay side by side, looking at the blue

sky above, their breathing slowly settling.

Finally Adam said, 'Jean, I'm sorry, I should never have started.'

She sat up, leaned over, stopped further talk with a kiss and began tidying herself up.

Whilst she did so he said, 'I'm not going to go there, do that again until you are really mine. I don't trust myself to know when to stop.'

Jean finished with her clothes, stood up and held out her hands. He took them and she helped to haul him to his feet. She looked up at him.

'Don't feel guilty — I started it — and I didn't want you to stop.'

★ ★ ★

They went to see the minister of the local church, and after a few deft questions as to her religious background, the banns were read at that Sunday's service, where she met many of the parishioners.

One evening he called his mother and father and spoke to them at great length, then came out of the study to where she was sitting in front of a log fire, Monty at her feet.

He beckoned.

'Come on, it's time to meet the parents

— they want to take a look at you.'

Startled, Jean shot up, causing Monty to bound to his feet and give a loud bark.

'They're here?'

He laughed, took her by the arm and led her into the study.

'We've got Skype rigged up. What do you think we are — primitive people?'

He sat her down in front of the screen, and there she faced a distinguished-looking man who rather reminded her of the old film star, Douglas Fairbanks Jnr, whom she had seen in many an old black and white movie on the Hollywood Greats channel.

'So, my dear, you are the one Adam speaks so eloquently about — and I can see quite clearly why.'

To her relief she found Charles Crawford warm and generous and easy to talk to, but became tense with anxiety as she was eventually told to wait while he changed places with Adam's mother.

The instant the latter came properly into view, Jean could see where Adam got his looks from, at least around the eyes.

Sarah Crawford was the epitome of a well-bred British woman, and had a refined but not affected voice.

But to Jean's surprise, she turned out to be very down to earth, with a wicked, dry sense of humour when it came to speaking about Adam.

'It'll do him good to have a woman take him in hand. He's jolly lazy and selfish like every man I've ever known.'

Behind Jean, Adam rolled his eyes.

'Oh Mother, not that old chestnut again.'

When Jean finally said goodbye and left him to finish off, she went back to the drawing room and settled on the sofa, pushing off her shoes and curling her feet up underneath her.

He finally came in smiling broadly.

'Glad that's over? Anyway, they really liked you — but I knew they would.'

Jean shook her head in disbelief.

'Darling, they were wonderful to me, considering they had no warning, must think I'm — '

He didn't want to hear the word 'gold-digger' again, so swiftly bent down and smothered her with kisses, then over-balanced and fell onto her.

Laughing they rolled to the floor, still kissing.

He nearly lost his resolve, would have, he realized, in the relief of having introduced Jean to his parents, but help was at hand. Monty, barking madly, joined in the fun, jumping on top of them.

Adam finally flopped back onto the sofa, head on a cushion and eyes closed as Jean stayed on the floor, sitting with her back to it, stroking and calming Monty. He said firmly, 'He's not coming on honeymoon with us, that's for sure.'

In her bed that night, looking out of the window at a night sky full of stars, Jean thought of the time she had spent there, of the warmth and loveliness of the people and of Adam.

They were all but married in name. Anywhere else she guessed, she would be downstairs now, sharing his bed, *their* bed.

But Adam was different.

And she had begun to learn just how stubborn a Scotsman could be.

18

In the run up to the wedding day they settled into a routine. Adam was always out early; Jean never saw him at breakfast, sometimes not all day. Other days he was home for a quick lunch.

She took to taking Monty for regular walks and helped out at the stables, where one of the young girls began to give her very tentative riding lessons — at first just how to get on and off, and sit properly, holding her heels down in the stirrups, then being led around the paddock.

The girl couldn't get over the fact that Jean, from Texas, couldn't ride a horse.

It was on one such afternoon when, after a cup of tea, as she was preparing to take Monty for his last walk before nightfall, that the bell that was operated by an old-fashioned, cast-iron pull outside the door, gave a couple of clangs.

She had freshened up and had just come down the first flight of stairs, dressed in jeans, her hair pulled back and with a minimum of mascara and lipstick. Jean had noticed that the skin on her face was losing its tanned

Texan look and was beginning to acquire a paleness, albeit with rosier cheeks. Against the modern trend it might be, but she was delighted: she was becoming a local. Scotland was going to be her home from now on, and women didn't look like wrinkled, baked potatoes, or spray-tanned from living and working indoors in the air conditioning all the time.

Jean turned onto the main landing hearing the murmur of men's voices coming up from the hall, then Mrs McAllister called out.

'Miss Sinclair, you have visitors.'

Puzzled, she took a last glance in a mirror she was passing, checking she was presentable. It could only be Adam's friends — she had been introduced to so many over the last two weeks — or something official. She frowned at that. It could be British Immigration — had she done something wrong?'

Either way, she wanted to present a good image. She tripped lightly down the red stair-carpet.

She recognized them before she reached the bottom. Smiling, they both turned to look up at her, and then Chris said, 'Good afternoon, Jean. My, you look radiant.'

Absolutely caught off guard, stunned, she couldn't hide her amazement.

'What are you two doing here?'

Beaming, Steve threw his arms wide.

'Hey, is that any way to greet old friends?'

She reached the bottom step, and paused. Something didn't feel right. It was weeks since she had last seen them.

'Hardly old friends, Steve, and besides you two disappeared without so much as a goodbye wave. What happened?'

Chris came nearer.

'Had a report about better fishing on another river. Couldn't waste time, could we? But we felt rather rotten leaving like that, so we decided to look you up before we went home.'

Even as Mrs McAllister asked, 'Would you like a cup of tea or coffee, gentlemen?' Jean's unease was beginning to mushroom.

Their previous meetings had only been brief; the longest was when they had bought her a drink that time. No way did it warrant them looking her up now, and in any case — the thought hit her like a freight train — how on earth had they got this address?

It must have shown in her eyes, because Steve moved over to stand right on top of Mrs McAllister who frowned at the closeness as he drawled in his Texas voice, 'No time for tea, ma'am.'

Jean took a step back up the stairs.

'How did you get this address? What's going on?'

And then it happened.

As Steve grabbed a screaming Mrs McAllister and Chris, with lightning speed that belied his heavy bulk, leapt up the stairs and seized her around the waist, effortlessly bringing her kicking and struggling back down to the hall floor, a figure stepped into the open front door.

The evening sunlight was behind him, so it took a second for her to realize who it was.

Don.

His voice was only just above a whisper as he said, 'How are you, Jean? You're looking a little wan, if I may say so.'

She stopped kicking and struggling. It was as if a rattler had struck her, leaving her in shock.

Mrs McAllister was trying to claw at Steve's face. Carefully, and with an air of professional training, he managed to restrain her, but then, because of the woman's continued screaming, he gave her a hefty cuff across the face. The elderly woman looked dazed, then sagged in his grip.

Everything went quiet except for the dull 'thonk' of the grandfather clock in the corner.

Don came further into the hall, nodded for Chris to set her down, and stood over her.

'Wasn't all that difficult to find you. The place is abuzz with the talk of the Yankee girl and the young Laird.'

He dragged out 'young Laird' in a sarcastic Scottish voice.

'And besides, the boys here have been working for me from the very beginning, so they knew where to start searching.'

She scowled at them, at the friendly, grinning Chris and the smiling Steve, who gave her a little cowboy salute with one finger from his forehead.

'You bastards.'

Chris tut-tutted.

'That's no way to sweet talk a police officer, ma'am — could run you in for that.'

Jean snorted.

'Police officer? You're just working for *him*.' She spat out the 'him' as she nodded at Don.

'Oh yes we are, ma'am — just earning a little extra bonus during our annual vacation — and enjoying the fishing too.'

Jean had to try, but in her heart of hearts, she guessed it wasn't going to be that easy.

'Well, if you want to keep your jobs, you'll let us go now, and get out of the country.'

She turned her attention to Don.

'What were you thinking of, sending them to spy on me? Why?'

Don towered over her, brutally grabbed her

chin with his finger and thumb, digging into her skin.

He raged into her face, showering her with spittle as he screamed, 'You silly little bitch. You don't think I was going to let you go just like that, to some limey bastard? You're mine — have been for a long time. And I've put up with your shit for long enough.

'What's mine, stays mine unless I say so. And with you, I don't say so — *bitch*. So you are coming back to the States with me, we're marrying, and that's an end to it.'

But he wasn't finished.

The tirade went on and on.

Jean felt his hot breath, could smell bourbon.

She realized in that moment that she had never really known him, how deranged he was. All his life he'd got what he'd wanted — from his parents, at college and so on.

Maybe her big attraction for him was that she had never just completely given into his demands.

Flashing through her mind was the recent revelation that he'd had one-night stands when he was away from home, and what of the girls?

That he could be rough, there was no longer any doubt. She wondered if they'd married, would she have become a battered wife? She had seen so many as a nurse, always saying they had slipped and fallen, when the clinical evidence showed otherwise.

Again and again.

Her body was trembling with terror, but something inside her knew that she had to stand up to him, not just for Adam, for happiness, but because if she didn't, she would never be herself again, would never have self-respect.

He would dominate her until there was nothing left of the Jean Sinclair that was. But now, he'd flipped. And she realized with a coldness that seemed to paralyze her body, that stopped it shivering, that he was capable of anything.

Even murder.

When he finally ceased abusing her she broke the silence with, 'So, what's happening now?'

Don shrugged. The heat seemed to have left him.

'You and me, we're getting a flight to Dallas tomorrow. Our wedding day is booked for Thursday. Then we'll have a little honeymoon. I thought the Cayman Islands would be just right. I've got a bit of business to do but otherwise it's very quiet.' He sniggered. 'We'll get to know each other real swell.'

Jean felt the bile rising in her throat, but managed to lift her chin defiantly.

'You're mad. What makes you think I'm going to agree with all that?' She raised her hand, and showed the ring on her finger. 'I'm engaged already. So I won't be on the plane, and I certainly won't be marrying you — you can't make me.'

Don frowned, and started to turn away, then came back and slapped her face. It was a stinging blow, and through the pain she tasted blood on her lip.

This time his voice was steady, matter of fact, which made what he said even more frightening.

'Should have done that a long time ago.'

It seemed to give him fresh impetus so he back-handed her, sending her head twisting violently the other way.

This time her cheek felt as if it was swelling, and her eyesight blurred for a moment.

He grabbed her around the throat, eyes fierce.

'Now listen up. You come now, or that lady' — he pointed at Mrs McAllister — 'gets hurt. And when we get to the States you will marry me, or this Scottish guy you've got the hots for gets hurt too — in his case, real bad.'

He moved his face so that it was almost touching hers.

'Might even be fatal.'

Jean felt the fight leave her, but she managed, 'You couldn't do all that.'

Don pulled back.

'Take it from me, Chris and Steve will think of something. They've done it before.'

He gave a humourless chuckle.

'Drown in Loch Ness, or better still, be half-eaten by the monster, eh, boys?'

She saw that the two of them didn't flinch, didn't protest. Jean realized then that they were capable of what he threatened, they were smiling at her in an oddly sinister manner.

As if to make sure she had understood, Don added, 'They're going to stay on, all expenses paid until after we're safely wed. Ain't that right, guys? So you see, until I contact them . . . '

He drew a finger across his throat.

There could be no doubt that he meant the gesture to indicate what would happen to Adam.

Jean prayed that it was all a nightmare, prayed that she would wake up sweating in her bed upstairs.

But it was real, was happening.

The groans coming from Mrs McAllister

made her realize that.

She could not think of a thing she could say or do that would matter to this monster before her.

She had thought she had known him so well. Did anyone truly ever know another human being in this life?

Then she thought of Adam.

And she knew, in a way that she had never felt with Don, that she did.

They were soulmates.

Faced with the ultimatum, with Mrs McAllister badly hurt and the unthinkable — Adam murdered by these men — all she could say was, 'I'll get my coat.'

Perhaps later she could get away and do something, but for the moment there was no other choice.

Don took her acquiescence for granted, and nodded to Chris.

'Go with her. Make sure she has her purse and passport.'

To Steve he said, 'Do something with the old girl. Find somewhere to lock her up and throw away the key. Make sure she hasn't got a cell phone. I've dealt with the landline.'

Steve frogmarched Mrs McAllister from room to room until he found Adam's study. It only had a small window, so even if the old girl managed to finally get out through it, it would take her a long time, and there was a drop to a basement level below.

He thrust her roughly into the desk chair, ripped out the phone and computer lines and swiftly wrapped some flex around her, binding her to the chair.

'There we are. Now you be a good granny — or I'll come back and hurt you — and you wouldn't want that, would you?'

Mrs McAllister looked petrified, and said, 'No, no — but please don't do anything to Miss Jean — please. I'll be good.'

Steve nodded.

'Knew you would see sense.'

With that he closed the door, turned the key.

Mrs McAllister waited with bated breath, and then heard the key being withdrawn. It was what she wanted; he had swallowed her pathetic act.

Immediately she started to wriggle. He hadn't made a good job of it. Soon she was out of the chair. Did he really think that that whimsy, helpless, pleading old woman was for real?

As they left, Steve carefully closed the front door behind them. Chris held Jean's elbow in a vice-like grip while Don walked on the other side of her as they marched across the gravel to a four-wheel-drive Jeep.

Jean said quietly to Don, 'If anything happens to Adam, I will *kill* you, you know that?'

His mouth turned up at the corner as he said, 'Then it's up to you to do as you're told — that way you won't have a reason to kill me, the father of your children, will you?'

The last bit took her breath away. God forbid, but of course, it would happen, he would see to that.

Sooner or later he would make her pregnant. Could she ever abort it? She knew the answer to that: No.

Thereafter she would be bound to him for the rest of her life, whatever happened. Children did that to a woman.

As she was sat between the two bulky Dallas cops in the back and Don got into the driving seat she asked, 'Where are we going? Glasgow?'

She guessed it would be to the nearest international airport.

Don started the engine, and moved off down the drive.

'Nothing so simple as that. You don't think I'm going to risk your Highland laddie somehow interfering, do you? A quick call to the police and then immigration? Wait and see.'

With that they turned out of the gate

— away from the road to Inverdee and Glasgow. Mystified and frightened, Jean took a last look at the house with its old stone and ivy-covered walls nestling in the trees with the hills behind.

It was all so cruel. If nothing else she was leaving her heart there. She wondered what Adam would do. He'd come after her for sure when he heard what had happened from Mrs McAllister. Her stomach ached with worry for his safety. And if he only reached her after the quickie wedding ceremony Don had planned, albeit done under duress, would he understand?

Did such marriages still stand if there had been an element of coercion, and how could she prove it? It would all seem so far-fetched to a District Attorney, and anyway, the DA was one of Don's circle.

Small town, backwater America.

Another fear swamped her.

Could she trust Don to keep his word? She had seen him mad with jealousy and possessiveness.

Later, he might have Adam killed whatever happened.

The car suddenly turned up a very small single-track road that led north, towards mountains on the skyline.

Where on earth was he taking her?

Mrs McAllister went straight to the top right-hand drawer of Adam's desk. In seconds she had the spare key, and even with her arthritic hands she had opened the door.

She ran as fast as she could back to the hall, but they had already gone.

For a woman of her age she moved with remarkable alacrity, straight up the stairs.

Puffing and wheezing, she ran to the big landing window overlooking the drive.

She saw the car at the gate but couldn't make out the number plate.

Although she had been dazed to begin with, she had recovered quicker than she had led them to believe, and soon understood Jean was being abducted against her will by the man referred to as Don, a nasty piece of work.

What Don and his overweight, to her mind, gangsters had not known, was that in a former life many years ago, Joan McAllister had been a WPC in the Grampian Force.

She was still quick-witted, and knew that she had to get as much information as possible on the bastards.

So she noted the car's dark blue colour, that it was a big off-road type — and, it staggered her, that it turned right, *away from* the direction of the town.

Swearing under her breath in Gaelic she went to a drawer in the small landing table and took out a pair of high-powered Zeiss binoculars, a relic of World War Two that Adam's father had liberated from a Panzer officer. The Laird used them for bird and deer watching and the like.

She thumbed the focus wheel, the trees blurring in and out until they were suddenly clear — the leaves seeming so big she could reach out and pluck them off the branch.

When she found the car it exploded into view, shaking with the fragility of her grip. Even with trees flashing past she could make out Jean in the back, sandwiched between the two overweight Americans.

'You poor wee lassie. They won't get away with it — the Laird will see to that. They won't know what's hit 'em.' More Gaelic followed that indicated that they were born out of wedlock, were piles of dung, were destined to roast in the fires of hell forever when they reached their maker — as surely they would.

All this was said as she tracked the vehicle, suddenly noting with a start that it had turned up a single track road that led nowhere — only to some stone huts in the foothills of the mountains used by the mountain rescue people and climbers.

She followed the vehicle's progress until it disappeared from view over a tree-lined ridge. There could be no doubt where they were heading.

She lowered the binoculars.

'Right, you scumbags, you're going nowhere.'

Mrs McAllister was a fan of American TV police dramas.

In her soft Highland accent, it sounded strange — and more threatening.

But for the moment she could do nothing. Nobody was around, or remotely near, and in any case, Master Adam was due here anytime now. He would know what to do, and he had his mobile phone.

19

It was dusk by the time Adam arrived back at the house from an all-day conference he'd chaired, held by the local regional tourist board.

His anticipation of seeing Jean again, followed by a quiet supper and afterwards sitting before a log fire and talking about the future, watching the glowing embers and the dog lying before it, sometimes anxiously raising his head as a log settled, before dropping back to the carpet, disappeared the moment his headlights swept the front of the house, and a distressed Mrs McAllister came running out to tell him the shocking news.

Inside, he sat her down and made her re-tell everything that had happened, sometimes stopping her to ask about every little detail she could remember. There were several things he wanted to be very sure about.

What was Jean like? Was she frightened or injured in any way?

The woman shook her head.

'She was a feisty wee lassie. She was slapped around by that one who says she has to marry him, but otherwise she's fine.'

The words 'slapped around' burnt into his heart, and began an anger in his blood that would have been recognized by his ancestors in the days of the clan feuds. There was only one way to relieve it.

The man would pay for it — with his own blood.

The second point he was keen on being sure about, was whether they were definitely armed like she said.

Mrs McAllister was adamant.

'I saw guns in holsters, like detectives on the TV, sir, under their jackets. They looked like ones I've seen in your daddy's cabinets in the past.'

His father once had an extensive collection of weapons that had been handed in during one of the police amnesty days, with several older pieces going to a museum.

'Are you sure? Foreigners carrying firearms in this country is illegal. They would have had difficulty bringing them in.'

She snorted. 'I don't know about that, sir, all I know is I saw them.'

Finally, he asked,

'Are you sure they headed up into the hills — not towards Glasgow?'

She was adamant.

'I followed the car, sir — saw her in the back.'

He struggled with that.

Why the hell should they have gone up there, a dead end, instead of making it as fast as possible out of the area, straight for an airport?

Mrs McAllister's impatience finally broke through.

'We must get the police, sir, get after them. Heaven knows what they'll do with Miss Jean.'

Adam Crawford's eyes narrowed. The thought of anybody hurting her was almost too much to handle.

But his training kicked in. He knew what he was going to do.

He held up the car keys.

'I'll ring them immediately, but I want you to go to Inverdee Police Station. Ask for Superintendent Patterson — or tell them to contact him at home. Tell them I said it was urgent. Tell him about the guns. That will automatically evoke a response — armed units will be sent from Glasgow.'

His housekeeper looked at him anxiously.

'What are you going to do, sir?'

He began to dial 999.

'I'm going to follow them on Betsy.'

Mrs McAllister was horrified.

'Oh, for God's sake, don't do anything rash, sir. These men are dangerous.'

He waved at her to get going.

'There's no way I'm going to leave Jean to their tender mercies — now *go*. It'll take a long time for the police to get their act together; we probably won't see any useful response until dawn.'

At that moment the operator answered, and asked which emergency service was required.

What nobody knew, not Mrs McAllister, nobody other than his parents and his sister who lived in Maidenhead, was that Adam Crawford had not only been in the Army; he'd volunteered and been accepted, trained, and fought for two years with the 22nd Regiment of the SAS — the Special Air Service. And he'd figured out what his enemy was up to.

Sometime early the next day, probably just after dawn, he was convinced that there would be a helicopter pick-up — something that had happened to him time and time again at the end of missions.

They would be whisked away to somewhere with another transatlantic airport, maybe Belfast or the Republic of Ireland, even Norway.

He worked swiftly, running up to his room, stripping off his clothes. From his wardrobe he took a pair of brown and green camouflage ex-Army combat trousers and pulled them on. They were followed by a similar Army jacket, with loose strips of extra cloth sewn all over it — his sniper's gear, which he used for deer stalking. Finally, he sat on the edge of the bed and put his feet into all-in-one rubber boots that had seen many a day and night clambering silently over the rugged mountains of Afghanistan, and began lacing them up.

From his firearms cabinet he took out a sporting rifle, checked its bolt action, then slid it into its long holster. Into his pockets he put two boxes of ammunition and slung a pair of night-vision goggles around his neck, another souvenir of his days hunting the Taliban.

He set off in a loping run for the stables. By the time he'd got Betsy out of her box, put on a saddle and reins and strapped the rifle in its holster into position, twenty minutes had elapsed.

Adam Crawford hoisted himself into the saddle, urged the horse forward with a click of his tongue and a quick flick of his heel.

Out on the road the light was fading fast. It was pitch black between the deep hedges. Occasionally he used his night-vision goggles, but when he turned off the road and struck out across country, there was more light. He urged Betsy into a gallop, intent on making as much speed as possible while he could. As it was, he was cutting miles off the route their 4×4 had taken on the winding, twisting track.

His mind was set on only one thing: getting Jean back safely into his arms.

And woe betide any man who got in his way.

20

It had taken over an hour to reach the end of the track, an hour of Jean being tossed from side to side on the back seat against the massive bodies of Chris and Steve as the car bumped and swung and creaked over the rutted surface.

Now she could see a stone building and another smaller one as they ground to a halt on an area of flat, sheep-grazed grass.

She was made to stay in the car with Don as the others checked that nobody was around and that the buildings were empty.

Chris came back, leant into the window.

'All clear.'

They got out, and then Don ordered, 'Tie her hands behind her back.'

Jean was aghast.

'That's not necessary. Where would I go out here?'

Don shook his head.

'I don't know, but with you, I can't take risks.'

Jean was contemptuous.

'And you say you love me?'

Don shrugged as Steve pulled her hands

roughly behind her and secured them at the wrists with a strip of plastic like she'd seen used on detainees on the news. It hurt.

They had come prepared for anything. She realized then just how much Don had planned and spent on getting her back.

It wasn't love; it was an obsession, bordering on madness.

Frightened and puzzled, she looked around at the black outline of the mountain in the last light in the sky, and the stone huts lit up in the headlights of the car.

'What are we doing here?'

Nobody replied as, with Don gripping her elbow, she stumbled to the door of the nearest building.

A new fear began to build in her, tightening her stomach till it felt like a cold block of ice was in there.

Perhaps Don had no intention of taking her back. Perhaps it was all a lie and he was going to end it here — after he'd done what he wished with her.

Maybe he would even let the others take a turn . . .

She began to shake with fear.

There could be no other explanation.

She already realized he was mad; perhaps she'd underestimated how completely deranged he'd become.

As if to confirm her worst fears there were several camp beds in the stone-walled room. She was pushed down onto one, but instead of what she dreaded, the men gathered around a paraffin stove.

Don got out a lighter, sparked it up and set fire to the wick.

Chris and Steve went outside again. She heard the car start up and then slowly being driven and parked somewhere else.

Jean guessed that they were hiding it from view.

Her heart was thumping in her chest so violently she feared it would rupture.

She waited as Don continued to fiddle with the stove, then she could contain herself no longer.

'What are we doing here? What are you going to do with me? Are you going to kill me?'

Hearing the words out loud made her convulse with shock.

Don straightened up, put a kettle on the now lit stove.

'What do you take me for — doing away with my own wife to be. I've told you what's going to happen.'

When she continued to look bemused he chuckled, came over and tried to tickle her under the chin, but she jerked her head away.

Frowning, he said, 'You're going home in style, honey. Helicopter, then first class all the way to good ol' Texicana.'

She was right. He'd spent a lot of time figuring out what he was going to do, and no expense was being spared in the effort. Goodness knew how much the bent cops were costing him, to say nothing of everything else. No doubt his father and the company would foot the bill, knowingly or unknowingly.

Quietly she said, 'You know I don't love you, Don, that my heart will always be with another?'

He shrugged.

'You'll come round. All this' — he waved at the little window — 'Scottish tomfoolery will pass. You're young; it's just a silly holiday romance.'

She stared back at him. He had no idea, or rather, didn't comprehend or understand anything about her, and Adam. Didn't care.

Don was so bound up in himself that he couldn't see, let alone accept, that it was over between them.

His pride was hurt, and like all macho men, he'd turned to violence.

Weirdly, she felt sorry for him — despite what he intended doing, what he had done so far.

And could she trust him to keep his word about not hurting Adam?

Knowing that he was alive would probably eat away at him. Then what?

She loved Adam so much she realized she would do anything to protect him — even if it meant the unthinkable.

If she killed Don, he would be safe — forever.

Killed? She was contemplating murder? My God, she thought, how she had changed in the last few weeks. Was that what love did to you?

But in so doing, she would never be the same woman again.

And worse.

Could Adam ever reconcile her with the innocent girl he had fallen in love with?

It was a cruel paradox.

With the one action she would save one life, but end two others; Don and her own.

For she would not wish to live without the love of Adam.

But the more she thought about it, the more convinced she became that Don was not to be trusted. She asked, 'When is the helicopter coming?'

'Half an hour after dawn.' He chuckled. 'Now you be a good wee lassie, as they say in this damp, God-awful place, and it will make things so much easier for yourself, and for that skirt-wearing jackass.'

'You promised you would leave him alone,' Jean said.

Don enjoyed the moment.

'That's right, but Chris and Steve are staying behind, don't forget. Once we're wed, they'll come home, I promise.

'But,' he gave her a look that said it all, 'they can always come back — anytime.'

She shook her head and tried one last time, appealing to his better nature.

'Please, Don. Why can't you just let go and part good friends? There's plenty of other girls who'd fall over to — '

His hand shot out, covered her mouth roughly, pressing her lips painfully onto her teeth.

'Shut up. You never know when to shut up. One squeak from you on the journey home, and you know what will happen.'

He let her go and pushed her so that she fell back onto the bed.

Still with her arms tied behind her, she rolled up into a foetal position, fearing more blows.

None came.

To think she was once set to willingly marry this monster. Her parents had seen beyond the superficial charm, had tried to discourage her, and quite uncharacteristically, had made it plain to Don that they did not care for him.

Her own vanity had blinded her to the signs of selfishness; she was so thrilled to have been chosen by the man considered most desirable at the college — one of the top jocks.

Well, she knew now what a disaster that would have been.

And in a cruel twist of fate it had taken the tragic loss of her mother and father and the trip over here to uncover his true personality.

An awful thought struck her, so awful that at first she tried to drive it from her mind. But having now seen the extent that Don was prepared to go to, she could not shake off the idea: did he have anything to do with her parents' death?

Tears began to trickle down her face. All she wanted in the world at that moment was for Adam's strong arms to hold her tight and safe.

In the little window above the bed, in the blackening sky, stars were beginning to show. But it would only be a few hours before dawn, this far north in summer.

She wondered what Adam was doing. He would have found out by now what had happened. Her hopes rose at the thought of him coming to rescue her soon.

And then a great heaviness overcame her.

There was no way he would guess they were here.

Don had thought of everything.

★ ★ ★

Adam had ridden some fifteen miles before he dismounted. He calculated that there were another three miles to the end of the track and the stone huts, which was just over a ridge.

From the saddle he took his hunting rifle, then gave Betsy an affectionate rub on the nose, and murmured, 'Home, girl, go home,' and then he gave her a gentle smack on the flank.

Snorting, Betsy dutifully ambled off into the darkness.

Using the night-vision goggles he scanned the way ahead, the pine trees and grassy areas standing out in various shades of luminescent green.

Satisfied as to where he was, he took them off and let his eyes grow accustomed to the night again before moving off.

There was only a crescent moon, but the sky was alive with stars glittering like millions of diamonds scattered on black velvet.

He moved silently, stopping frequently, dropping to his haunches, listening, sniffing and checking for any movement. A gentle breeze ruffled the foliage by his head as he reached the edge of the ridge. Cautiously, on his stomach, he moved out of the tree-line and looked across the plateau.

Straight away he saw the stone huts, and a faint glimmer of light.

He settled down and put on the night-vision goggles. The faint light in the window suddenly became a shift of bright intense green, like a flare.

Quickly, he swung away from it, swept the stone buildings and the immediate surroundings. He found the car very quickly, probably easier than in the daytime, its rear reflectors picking up the faint light more than the greenery around it.

He could see it was as Mrs McAllister had described.

He breathed out his satisfaction with a quiet, 'Yes'.

He spent several minutes examining the terrain, and was just able to make out the big painted 'H' contained in a circle marking the helicopter pad for use by the emergency services.

He made particular note of the undulations in the land around the stone buildings and the nearest bushes, tracking in his mind the shadows that would form in the early morning light.

When he was finished, he had pinpointed the position he would take up — before he struck — and that would depend on when the chopper arrived. It was the one variable he could not assess, but he guessed it would be early.

Satisfied, he shrank back into the pitch-blackness of the trees to wait.

But it was difficult.

She was so near.

Was she being ill-treated?

It needed all his self-discipline and training to stay his hand.

But it would be no good charging in there right now.

Apart from the danger to her, this was no Hollywood movie and he was no superhero, firing two guns at once with amazing accuracy.

There were three of them to his one.

Surprise might balance things up if he was lucky, but the third man might easily take him down.

Or her.

Adam Crawford had seen the results of indiscriminate shooting in a confined space, and it wasn't pleasant.

Shooting? Would it really come to that? But they were armed, so he had to assume they would be prepared to use their guns.

He spent the remaining hours of darkness, resting up, but keeping a watchful eye on the area.

Finally, checking the time, and with the knowledge that dawn was less than half an hour away, he stirred. Using the night-vision goggles he collected a pile of twigs and foliage, then took off his jacket and began inserting them through holes in the strips of camouflage that hung loose from the material, especially on his back. When he was finished and had put it back on, the effect when he was lying face down would be like a clump of rough scrub.

He found a patch of moist earth, and began spreading it all over his face, until only a rim of white skin showed around his eyes.

The eastern sky began to lighten. Adam moved out of cover, the rifle now free of its protective cover, held two-handed before him.

He took a wide path around the huts, came up to the place he had selected from a very different direction than the track that led back to Inverdee.

Slowly he sank to the ground, twisting his way into the soft earth, and pulled some thistles and long grass over him.

It wasn't as good as a properly prepared sniper or observer position he'd used in the Army, but it would do for this bunch of amateurs. All he needed was to not be seen immediately. They would be looking skyward while the pilot concentrated on them and the landing zone.

Satisfied, he racked a shell into the breech of the rifle, put his eye to the telescopic sight and took a practice sweep at the rapidly emerging buildings that were now catching the first warm rays of the rising sun.

All was ready.

Now for the waiting game he had played so many times before.

He thought of what he might have to do. He had killed several times as a professional soldier in the service of his Queen and country, but this was different.

The safety of Jean was his prime concern, and if that meant killing, so be it.

But this time, for whatever good reason, it would be murder — justified or not.

But if she was in mortal danger, he knew he would not hesitate.

21

Nobody had slept. Propped against the stone wall Chris and Steve had occasionally closed their eyes, but Jean was acutely aware that they would be alert in seconds at the slightest sound. Mercifully, nobody had touched her, not even Don, lost in the dark shadows in the corner. But she was sure his eyes were boring into her.

Slowly, at first, the dawn light began to show in the little window. Soon, it was quite daylight.

Chris stood up.

'I'm going for a pee.'

Jean rolled her feet onto the floor.

'I need to go as well.'

'No.' Don's face emerged from the shadow. 'She'll try something.'

Chris shook his head.

'Don't be a creep, man, the little lady is going nowhere, and besides we've got to release her arms; this helicopter pilot ain't going to like the look of that.'

Don shook his head.

'Don't worry about him, he's being paid enough.' Eventually, he conceded. 'Watch her like a hawk.'

Jean, held by Chris at the elbow, stumbled, blinking, outside. He took her round the side of the building.

'Wait there.'

When he'd finished he released the plastic binder on her wrists. Her hands were so numb, her fingers could hardly pull at the zipper of her jeans.

He grinned.

'Need any help there?'

Jean, guessing that Chris hadn't brought her out because of the goodness of his heart.

'I'll manage. Turn your back.'

When they came back around to the front, Don and Steve were out, scanning the sky.

At first she could hear it but not see it, the thumping roar of the helicopter engine, sometimes loud, then fading as it reverberated off the rocky cliffs or was absorbed by the forests.

It grew steadily louder.

'There it is.'

Chris had seen it first. Seconds later, Jean could just make out the tiny object — she'd been looking too high. It was coming in low and fast between the mountains.

Rapidly the black speck grew, became a long sleek helicopter that roared over them with a noise that battered her ears, before it climbed away, slowed, turned and began a steady descent onto the marked area.

She read, Donegal Western Air Services on its side.

Wind tugged violently at their clothes, her hair wrapping around her face.

Don grabbed her arm and shouted into her ear.

'Tell them nothing, you understand? Nothing.'

When she didn't immediately reply he shook her roughly, and yelled, 'Understand?'

Jean knew that once she was in that aircraft, it was the beginning of the end.

Perhaps it would be better to die, right there, on the land of her ancestors, mourned by the man she loved.

She was steeling herself to do something when a miracle happened.

Out of the corner of her eye — all of their eyes — a menacing figure reared up like some creature from the stuff of nightmares.

And in its hand, pointing unwaveringly at them, was the biggest rifle she had ever seen.

The engine noise died back, diminished to only the continuing swish of the rotor blades as a voice she instantly recognized, barked, 'It's over. Drop your weapons — careful and slowly.'

The two cops looked at each other,

knowing at once that the guy was trouble — professional trouble. The rifle that was unwaveringly pointed at them would blow a hole the size of a silver dollar if he fired. And as yet they had no idea if he was alone, that there weren't more behind them.

Steve took the lead.

'Okay, easy, pal.'

They slowly pulled out their pistols from their shoulder holsters, holding them between finger and thumb, then bending at the knees to drop them onto the grass.

The rifle was still trained on them.

'Now your back-ups.'

They looked at each other; the guy knew what he was doing.

The helicopter rotor blades continued to swish around as they reached for the smaller guns strapped to their ankles.

But suddenly, just as they finished, a revolver appeared in Don's hand, was pressed to Jean's temple.

'Drop the rifle — *now.*'

Adam swung it so that it was pointing straight at Don's head.

The rotors swished by.

He could do it, he was a fine shot.

But it was a hell of a risk — unthinkable.

If Don's fingers involuntarily twitched

when the bullet smashed into his brain . . .

Twenty seconds passed. Jean, terrified, had stopped breathing.

Swish, swish.

Quietly, Adam spoke to Chris and Steve, never taking his eyes off his target.

'You boys leave now, take this piece of shit with you — no harm done. Better than thirty years in Barlinnie gaol. They don't like ex-cops in there; what they'll make of Yank cops I hate to think . . . '

The rotor blades continued to swing around.

Suddenly the helicopter door opened and an Irish voice shouted, 'Are you'se coming or what? We haven't got all day if you want to make that connection at Shannon.'

Chris and Steve looked at each other, the latter nodding.

'It's a fuck-up, all right. Reckon we'd better accept the gentleman's offer.'

Don found himself surrounded, with a large hand closing over the pistol. Gently, it was taken from him, Steve's outstretched arm dangling the weapon between his finger and thumb, before letting it fall to the ground.

Jean tried to break free, but Don seized her around the throat. In seconds he was whirled around, slammed face first into the fuselage of the helicopter, and his arms pulled painfully up his back.

Without another word the two cops bundled him into the helicopter, then Chris climbed in, followed by Steve. Just before he closed the door, he turned, gave a two-fingered salute from his temple.

The door closed, and as Jean ran to Adam, the whooshing blades increased their speed and the engine roared, exhaust blowing the hot smell of burnt kerosene over them.

Ducking, they ran back, well clear, then held onto each other as, blasting the grass flat, the helicopter rose straight into the air then dipped its nose and roared forward and upwards into a climbing turn.

It passed over them.

In seconds the deafening noise dropped to a distant thumping as it skimmed away, all the while climbing higher towards the mountains.

When Chris, Steve and Don looked down, they saw two things:

In the far distance the flashing blue lights of a police convoy.

And nearer, standing defiantly, legs apart, on an outcrop of rock, Adam Crawford, one hand holding the barrel of the hunting rifle with the stock firmly planted on the ground, the other around the waist of a wild, auburn-haired woman, whose arms were both tightly around his waist, her head against his chest: a Highland chieftain, monarch of all he surveyed.

22

The wedding banns lasted three weeks. One week later they were married in the little stone-weathered church in Inverdee, where her mother had said, 'Yes' to her father.

Jean wore a cream silk wedding dress that had been in Adam's family for a hundred years, her hair pinned up in a chignon and sewn with wild flowers fresh from the fields.

Kath was her bridesmaid, in a modern green silk suit, and there was a pageboy — one of Mrs McAllister's nephews, in a white shirt with a ruffle, a kilt, and calf-length socks and black shoes. He staggered behind Jean, holding her short train. Every now and then Kath had to help him out.

The rows of pews were filled by estate workers, Mrs McAllister and a crowd of her friends and some colleagues of Adam's from the City of London, with their wives and girlfriends.

In the front row were his parents, *Sir* Charles — Jean had only found that out when she saw the invitation cards — and Lady Crawford, who had flown in the day before.

They all stood as the organ struck up the

Wedding March, and, on the arm of Angus who was giving her away, they made their way to where Adam stood, dressed magnificently in the kilted uniform of his old regiment.

He turned and smiled at her through her veil. Jean thought she would die with happiness. He looked so handsome, his face caught in the rays of light coming through the stained-glass window behind the altar.

All she could subsequently remember of the service was saying, 'I do', and Adam slipping the ring onto her finger.

When they came out into the sunlight behind a piper playing *Scotland the Brave,* they were confronted by past and serving officers of Adam's old regiment, all in kilts, forming an arch of swords.

After the photographs they all adjourned to the hotel, the same hotel that she had first stayed at in Scotland only a few months ago, which now seemed as if it had been somebody else's life.

They rode in an open-topped motor car from the 1930s, the 'V' shape of white ribbon folded around the great mascot on the radiator.

It smelt of old leather, something Jean would always associate with the most wonderful day of her life.

And there was another reason that had

enabled her to enjoy the day so much, even though she had initially greeted the news with a mixture of relief, and horror. Nothing was ever simple in their life.

She had been haunted from the moment Adam had rescued her with a nagging fear that Don would not let things rest, that he would come back, do something awful.

Now, though, that would never happen. News had reached her that he had been tragically killed in a car wreck, driving away from Dallas Fort Worth airport.

Investigators had concluded that, tired and jet-lagged, and drunk, he had lost concentration after a vacation to Scotland, where they drove on the other side of the road.

Ironically, two Dallas police officers who had also been on a fishing vacation in Scotland, were the first on the scene, but could do nothing.

It was that bit that had made her shiver. But they would be no threat to her — or Adam.

But she was sad.

Don had been a pig — worse, a psychopath. She remembered his attempted rape.

But the death of another human being was never a moment for rejoicing.

She clung to Adam as they took to the floor

for the first dance, feeling the safety of his strong arms around her, something she knew she would never be tired of, not even when they were in their nineties, living in a world that would no doubt be so different from this glorious day.

And night.

They left the reception to get changed. Kath helped her off with the wedding dress, and then Jean stepped out of her underwear and took a quick shower while Kath carefully put the dress back into its protective cover.

As she was sitting in her bra and panties, fixing her makeup, she could not stop shooting glances at the wondrous thing of beauty on her finger — the plain band of gold, the ring Adam had put there only hours ago.

It was like a miracle.

Adam, in a dark blazer, open sports shirt and cavalry twill trousers came knocking on the door just as she finished dressing, putting on a matching silk jacket over an olive-green dress.

Adam just stood there, not taking his eyes off her as she slipped on matching shoes.

'Well?' She came over to him. He put his hands on her waist, resting them on her hips.

'You look stunning.'

They just brushed their lips together before

going out onto the landing.

As they came down the stairs a great cheer went up, and shouts and whistles.

They said goodbye to his parents — Sarah Crawford fixing Adam with a fierce look.

'You be good to her now, Adam, or you'll have me to answer to.'

His father shook his hand, his other on his shoulder as he said, 'If Jean makes you half as happy as your mother has me, you'll be a lucky man — and I think she's just the girl for you.'

'Thanks, Dad, I *know* she is.'

They drove out of the hotel grounds in the open-topped car they'd arrived in, only this time there was a great tail of tin cans tied to the back bumper, crashing and bouncing on the ground above the 'Just Married' placard stuck to the spare wheel.

The car stopped at the house. Waiting for them was another car and a driver to take them to Glasgow, and the hotel Adam had booked before they flew off to Barbados the next day. He'd drunk far too much to drive them himself.

After that, they were coming back to set up home in a cottage on the estate. Jean had even got a temporary job with a local doctor as a nurse-receptionist, before retraining for a hospital appointment.

As Adam said, until she got pregnant.

By the time they reached the hotel, it was very late. Shown to their room, after he'd tipped the porter, Adam pulled off his jacket and flopped back onto the double bed.

Jean felt the warmth coming into her cheeks. The double bed — *their* double bed, their *first double bed.*

She took off her own jacket, and then retired to the bathroom. When she came out hc was still where she had left him, eyes closed.

Jean slipped off her shoes, went over to him. He looked to be fast asleep.

It was not what she was expecting, but he'd worked so hard all day that she took pity on him. He needed a night's rest.

They'd waited so long, what was one more night? The only thing to do was to make him more comfortable.

Gently she undid his shoes, pulled them off and set them quietly on the carpet, then she removed his socks. His toes were long and surprisingly slim. She couldn't resist placing her hands on the soft skin of his ankles, running her fingers lightly up and down.

She stopped herself, and got on with the job.

She released some buttons of his shirt, revealing more of the dark hair spreading down and across his chest. Although she was a nurse, her fingers fumbled a little — it wasn't the same as when she was a professional on duty.

His eyes opened, looked at her in a daze.

'Adam?' Her voice was husky. 'Do you want to get undressed?'

He didn't seem to have heard, still looking up at her in a dream, for all the world like an obedient little boy. Despite his masculine strength he suddenly looked very vulnerable.

She left the shirt, it would be too much effort and would wake him up if she tried to pull it over those powerful shoulders.

But the trousers she wasn't sure of at all. She had removed lots in her time, but of course they had always been patients, many in pain. This was something again.

Jean swallowed as her hand moved to his hard, flat stomach. Her tongue ran slowly over her lips, like a little girl opening a present, as she took hold of the leather belt and unhooked it, then unclipped the waistband of the trousers.

Gingerly, she pulled down the zip, and started to drag the garment off, trying but failing to avert her eyes as she struggled with the surprising tightness, but then realizing why when she noticed the reaction her manoeuverings had caused.

'Adam,' she said reprovingly, pulling his trousers free and throwing them aside, 'go to sleep — you need it.'

He didn't reply but there was a lazy smile around his mouth. Suddenly, he reared up, reached around her, and began to unzip her dress.

Her breath caught in her chest.

'Adam — you're tired! We can wait — we've done for so long that one more night will make no difference.'

Chuckling he said, 'I'm feeling better.'

The zip reached the small of her back. He brushed her shoulders and the dress floated to the floor. Jean leaned forward kneeling on the bed with her hands either side of him saying softly, 'Lie back down.'

His gaze was riveted to the sight of her breasts, suspended just above him inside the filmy lace of her bra.

He started to run the back of his fingers over each side, seeing the tips harden.

Jean swallowed, ordered, 'Take it off!'

He slid his hands around her and unclipped the back. The bra fell off, releasing her breasts.

She leaned further forward, held his arms at the wrists on the bed, knowing that he could easily overpower her if he wanted to.

But he didn't.

Jean let her hardened nipples play on the solid muscle and hair of his chest.

She closed her eyes in ecstasy.

When she eventually opened them it was to look down at his face beneath her.

'Adam — please.'

He teased her.

'What, Jean? What do you want?'

'Please,' she gasped.

There could be no doubt what she wanted — an end to her torment. Effortlessly he pushed her back, lifted her to the floor, then took his shirt off. As she stood there she could hardly breathe at the thought of what was coming.

He ran his hands lightly down the sides of her body to the top of her lace panties. With torturing slowness he slid them off, down over her thighs until they dropped of their own volition to the floor.

Jean stepped out of them and seized his briefs, releasing his caged manhood as she dragged them hungrily off. It was the signal for them to go for each other like a starving couple falling on a banquet. For a second their arms entangled as if they were fighting, then he pulled her down onto him and rolled over, so that he lay on top of her, his naked body dominating her naked body.

This time there was no pain, no anger, no

thoughts of revenge — just the culmination of weeks of absence, when they had longed for each other when both had thought all was lost.

Jean abandoned herself totally, felt herself flying; wild, free, to the heights of fulfilment, hardly hearing herself as she finally screamed out her joy at the summit of her passion, clinging to his thrusting body as she took it into herself, until the final explosive release that came again, and again, and again.

Afterwards they didn't speak: there was no need. Curled in his arms she was soon asleep; a sleep that was free of longing, of worry, of everything.

Deep.

Untroubled.

She was home at last, safe in his arms.

And unknown to them both the miracle of life was taking place, deep inside her belly; in her womb.

The cells fused, the genetic material merged, the Johnsons and the Crawfords were united at last.

Truly Adam was her, and she was Adam.

And they slept on.

We do hope that you have enjoyed reading this large print book.

Did you know that all of our titles are available for purchase?

We publish a wide range of high quality large print books including:
Romances, Mysteries, Classics
General Fiction
Non Fiction and Westerns

Special interest titles available in large print are:
The Little Oxford Dictionary
Music Book
Song Book
Hymn Book
Service Book

Also available from us courtesy of Oxford University Press:
Young Readers' Dictionary
(large print edition)
Young Readers' Thesaurus
(large print edition)

For further information or a free brochure, please contact us at:
Ulverscroft Large Print Books Ltd.,
The Green, Bradgate Road, Anstey,
Leicester, LE7 7FU, England.
Tel: **(00 44) 0116 236 4325**
Fax: **(00 44) 0116 234 0205**

Other titles published by
The House of Ulverscroft:

SCENT OF MADNESS

David Wiltshire

As Lieutenant Tom O'Hara investigates several gruesome murders in a large teaching hospital, a wave of terror about the escalating severity of the situation is sweeping through the nursing staff. Despite the obscene dissection of the victims' bodies, there are forensic clues pointing to the killer. O'Hara suspects a soldier who was brought back from Afghanistan in a coma. The man is the victim of a torture he associates with the scent of roses, worn by a sinister and unseen woman. The scent, unfortunately, is identical to that worn by Dr Jean Hacker, who works at the same hospital . . .

THE WOUNDED HEART

David Wiltshire

There was no doubt in Lt Mike Gibson's mind that he was going to die. As a lieutenant in the Royal Army Medical Corps, death and carnage had been with him every day from the beaches of Normandy to the crossing of the Rhine. One moment eclipsed all others, in a forest clearing in Germany, where he had the experience of hell on earth. He owed his life to one woman, Lily de Howarth, the woman he adored. And now he was planning to kill her in the name of love . . .